THE K-PRO

A CONTEMPORARY ROMANCE

M PEPPER LANGLINAIS

ALSO BY M PEPPER LANGLINAIS

Changers: Manifesting Destiny

Brynnde: A Regency Romance

Faebourne: A Regency Romance

The Fall and Rise of Peter Stoller

ON AUDIO

Brynnde: A Regency Romance

The New Sherlock Holmes Adventures

ALSO BY M PEPPER LANGLINAIS

Changers: Manifesting Destiny

Brynnde: A Regency Romance

Faebourne: A Regency Romance

The Fall and Rise of Peter Stoller

ON AUDIO

Brynnde: A Regency Romance

The New Sherlock Holmes Adventures

PROLOGUE

The torch is the only light in a sea of darkness, and the goddess holding it stands in its glow, beautiful and terrible in the way of goddesses, her hair the same gold as the flame, her dress a marvelous white. She waits, knowing they will come because they always come—there is always someone wanting something, needing a door unlocked, a path revealed.

"Trivia."

She turns. This is not who she expected, though she cannot be surprised except by how quickly he has caught up to her.

"We're back to my Roman name," she muses. "You must have been visiting your mother."

He ignores this; it does not signify. "You have something of mine," is all he says.

"I need it for my work," she tells him.

They stand on either side of the light, and she peers at him, past the flame and into the eyes that are the color of an oncoming storm.

"You cannot keep it," he tells her.

"I only look to borrow it," she says.

Even from the shadows, she can sense his frown. "For how long?"

"...Indefinitely."

He reaches for her, but she is too canny to be caught. She inverts the torch, extinguishing the fire, and before he can lay hands on her, she runs.

1

The scent of the hydrangeas carried across the wide lawn, pushed along by the ocean breeze. The combined smell of flowers and salt water, along with the remainder of uneaten dinner littering the table and the musk of wine on everyone's breath, was enough to turn David's stomach. He sat back and watched the sky grow steadily darker, idly wondering how long he was expected to stay.

No one tried to talk to him. Everyone here knew him too well for that, thank God. They'd been filming for a week and staying in the house—well, the principals had been staying in the house; the rest were in trailers or local hotels—but soon they would finish with this bit and move on to another location. In the meantime, nearly everyone was looking at this as a sort of paid holiday. Everyone but David, who took the work too seriously to relax. He'd been an actor for eight years, but most people wouldn't know it since he'd only begun to be noticed over the past two or three. His working philosophy was to keep his head down and barrel forward, ever building what looked to become a fair-sized empire if his luck continued.

"David Styles," said Alfred from across the table, drawing the words out so the name was long and somehow heavy. There were more wine stains in front of Alfred's seat than anywhere else on the white linen cloth. "What are you thinking about over there?"

Well, *almost* everyone knew him too well to try striking up a conversation. Or more likely, Alfred knew perfectly well and simply didn't care.

"Tomorrow's scenes," David said.

"Rehearsing your lines?"

David made a noncommittal noise and pushed back his chair. "Early call."

"Beauty sleep," sniffed Alfred. "Who needs it? Let the makeup artists earn their keep."

On Alfred's other side, Liz turned. "They earn their keep on you even when you've had enough sleep," she told Alfred, and he laughed, too long and too loudly.

David stood and heads swung his way. A chorus of "good night" rained around him. No one tried to stop him, to talk him out of leaving. He exited the patio, now reliant on the lanterns that lined its margins, and went inside to be enfolded by the warm, dim glow of chandeliers and the chill of too much air-con.

It was a lovely house, an old and grand estate that was as much a movie star as David had ever wanted to be. In fact, the damn house probably had more credits than David did. *But not for long*, he told himself. No, he was on the rise now; after this project there were three others in the wings, and his agent had new scripts for him to look at almost daily. He should be pleased. He *was* pleased. His life was turning out to be everything he'd aspired to.

But as he trudged up the richly carpeted stairs, David felt

tired. Overextended. He needed a real holiday, he supposed, and reasoned that maybe he'd finally reached a point in his career when he could afford to take one without missing any opportunities.

Did he have any down time between this project and the next? He'd ask Walter in the morning.

He reached his room, a nice room with big windows but no balcony. He wasn't the lead, after all. It was an ensemble cast but, unlike Alfred or Liz, his name wouldn't even be above the title. Not yet. Not this movie, and maybe not the next, but that was coming. That, and the room with the balcony, and creative input on the scripts, a producer credit... All of it was on the horizon.

But for now, this would do. Even though he'd showered before dinner, David hopped in again. He couldn't sleep without having showered first. Quirk. Kind of thing that would turn up in a magazine one day. He made it quick, pulled on clean boxers and went to lie down. Alone.

Not that it had to be that way; David had come far enough that he had good chances of company in bed when he wanted it. But besides his desire to remain focused when on a shoot, David found sex to be like rich foods—too much indulgence gave him a sour stomach. That, and almost a decade with Marjorie had made him the relationship equivalent of lactose intolerant. He'd only shaken her loose a year ago (had it been a year already?)—his broadening prospects necessitated keeping his options open—and if there was a tiny amount of guilt preventing him from moving forward on that front, David supposed that was normal. He'd get over it and so would she. Better to have done it now than when his career really started snowballing. Then it would have been so much tabloid fodder. He'd done them both a favor, really, breaking it off when he did.

These are the things David told himself as he drifted off

to sleep, alone in the oversized bedroom of an old English estate house that was serving as the shooting location for a movie in which he was, if not *starring*, at least majorly featured.

Name on the poster. Second to last, but they were alphabetical. Not much he could do about that aside from possibly change his name.

David Styles.

No, that was good. Easy to say, and no one was likely to misprint it.

And Margie had been proud of him, she'd said as much, and a little bit jealous of David's growing popularity, though she'd never said that of course.

David wasn't aware of having fallen asleep until he woke up. His last coherent thought had been along the lines of how stupid it was Margie had spelled her full name with a "j" but her nickname with a "g," something that had always bothered him. And as he opened his eyes (the handful of existing fan sites having reliably informed him that his clear blue eyes were his best feature), he imagined for a moment that Margie was there, in the bed. But no. She wasn't.

Margie was blond, you see. The head sharing David's pillow was auburn.

Startled, David jerked backward and came perilously close to falling off the mattress altogether. The girl—woman—lying next to him didn't move. She just stared, and for a terrible second David thought she might be dead. But the eyes tracked him. Strange eyes, a sort of acid green in color shot through with gold. Had to be contact lenses, David thought; no one had eyes like that in life.

He might have asked her who she was, that would probably have been more polite, but as he clambered the rest of the way off the bed the first words out of his mouth were, "What are you doing here?"

She blinked. "Someone called me."

"Well, it wasn't me."

She just kept staring.

"You've got the wrong room," David insisted, enunciating each word to make sure he was understood. He was beginning to wonder if she were mental, if this were his first encounter with a rabid fan. The idea was both terrifying and exhilarating.

She sat up, and David noticed she was dressed, at least, in a purple tie-dye singlet and denim skirt. More dressed than he was. Suddenly he felt exposed. But climbing back under the bedclothes wasn't an option, so despite his reluctance to turn his back on her, he went to the big wooden wardrobe and fetched the robe. "Oh, I know what this is!" he said as he belted the terrycloth around him. All at once it made perfect sense. "Alfred sent you, is that right? His idea of a joke."

"I only go where I'm called," she said.

So she *was* mental. David glanced around for his mobile phone. The house had security, didn't it? While his eyes darted over what suddenly seemed to be an inordinate number of surfaces in the room—little tables, the mantel over the fireplace, an old-fashioned vanity—he tried to keep her talking. That's what they did in movies, kept them talking. Because as long as they were talking they weren't, oh, tying you up and molesting you.

"What's your name?" he asked, turning a circle. A black phone in a mostly white room shouldn't have been so difficult to find.

"Cassandra," she said then gave her head a tiny shake as if to clear it. "Andra, though, really." She was watching him with a little frown on her face, and that irritated him. As if *he* were the one who was somehow untrustworthy, unstable.

"And what do you, uh, do?" David asked.

"I'm a K-Pro. It's over here, by the way." She gestured to

the marble-topped table on the far side of the bed. There sat his mobile. He would have to get past her to get to it.

"What's that?" David edged toward the foot of the bed with the thought of getting around it. "Like a grip or something?"

Andra's frown deepened. "A what?"

"You're on the set crew?" David persisted. He was at the corner of the bed.

"No."

"Work for the house then?" Center of the foot of the bed now.

She was watching him like a cat would watch a bird hopping across the lawn. Any moment she might pounce at him.

"You want me to hand it to you?" Andra asked.

David stopped. It could have been a trick, a reason for her to get closer. She'd act as if she were handing him the phone and then grab him.

But he was much taller than she was. He thought, anyway. Difficult to tell how tall she might actually be when she was sitting on his bed. But she was slender. Fit, from what he could see, but could she be stronger than him? Seemed unlikely.

Andra sighed and David flinched when she moved to reach over for the phone. "Here," she said, "catch."

2

L ess than twenty-four hours prior, Andra had been home in New Orleans. She'd spent the past five months there, in fact, which was longer than usual. Not because she didn't have any work to do—the flashes made her increasingly aware that she did—but because she'd been stalling on this one.

To be fair, she might have procrastinated regardless of her... What were they? Clients? Not exactly, but there was no other good name for them either. She was exhausted, after all, having just spent several months in New York with a pop star and almost a year before that in San Francisco with an aspiring artist. Andra felt it was only reasonable that she get some time to herself and a chance to indulge in some Creole cooking. No matter where she went in the world, no other place could get the jambalaya quite right. And forget about finding a decent po'boy.

But as ever, ignoring the flashes and dreams hadn't worked. They had only become more persistent, until it seemed even the ghost of her great-grandmother was hanging over her shoulder and urging her on. So after a few weeks of research she had booked a flight to London and a coach bus ticket out to this estate, only to arrive in the middle of the night. Not that that had been a problem; it worked out well enough for slipping inside and following the silent weeping to the person for whom she'd come.

They didn't always cry. Many of them were screaming on the inside, a number of them sang, a few were even laughing. And some sounded like nothing more than a sort of static or buzzing. Ambition and desire came in strange packages.

He'd been asleep, of course, this David Styles, but Andra's inner clock had been all thrown off, and exhausted but unable to sleep, she'd climbed onto the bed and simply lay there listening to the things going on inside him.

It hadn't been, in retrospect, the best way to get started, and Andra still wasn't sure what had caused her to go about it that way. Normally she would have met the client some-where public, conveniently run into them at a park or a museum or even turned up in a business meeting. But she'd known from the start this one would be different, and she knew deep down that was the reason she'd put it off as long as she had.

But she'd flustered him. And Andra couldn't blame him for being out of sorts, though she was acquainted with plenty of actors who would have been more pleased than upset to find a strange woman in their beds. David Styles was not one of those kinds, though; even the little bit she'd been able to discover online had told her as much. And what Andra didn't understand—and perhaps this was what bothered her—is what he wanted.

Well, no, she knew what he wanted on the surface. It was the same as many actors and musicians and writers and entrepreneurs she'd worked with. But he didn't need a K-Pro to succeed, so far as Andra could see; he was well on his own way.

So why was he calling out to her?

As David fumbled the phone she tossed him, she asked him outright, "What do you want?"

Divided between attempting to discreetly text Walter for help and keeping an eye on the crazy woman in his bed, David asked, "What do you mean?"

"It's okay, I'll wait 'til you're done," Andra told him.

"No, I just… I—" David had the sudden, uneasy notion he was somehow being rude. And the way the woman lifted her eyebrows when he looked at her did nothing to dispel this feeling. It was the same reproving motion his mother made when she caught him being impolite and expected him to apologize and behave.

But then he gathered his wits and decided this stranger was the one in the wrong, turning up in his bed uninvited. "Now look," said David, using the tone his headmasters had always taken, "you shouldn't be here. I won't get you in any trouble if you—"

He was interrupted by a knock at the door. "Mr. Styles?"

David looked at the woman on his bed. She continued to stare back with that infuriatingly expectant expression.

The door opened and Henry poked his blond mop around the jamb. "Walter said you—Oh, I'm sorry. I didn't know you had, er… Should I…?"

Good God, why had Walter sent Henry? He was a good enough lad for little errands, but this situation needed a knowledgeable hand. David didn't want this in the tabloids any more than he would have wanted a public breakup with Margie.

And now, of course, Henry had seen the girl—woman—and even if David swore him to secrecy there were no assurances Henry wouldn't let something slip. The boy meant well, David knew, but was clumsy in more ways than one.

Still, worth a try. "Not a word, Henry," David said, and

Henry's eyes became wide and round like a child who had been presented with a dessert cart before dinner. "There's been some kind of confusion, and I need Walter to help sort it out."

Henry nodded and retreated, leaving the door ajar in his haste. David sighed and his shoulders slumped. It was useless; the whole set would know within the hour, which meant any third-rate entertainment journalist looking for a tidbit would know shortly thereafter. It wouldn't be a head-line—David wasn't that big a star yet—but it would merit a couple paragraphs somewhere.

David turned back to Andra who continued to watch him keenly. And suddenly he understood that this was no fanat-ical interest; she was looking for something. Something specific.

"What?" he demanded.

"I don't get it," she said. "What do you *want*?"

"Your leaving might be a good start," David told her. "Not that it does me any good now. Fifteen minutes ago maybe."

"You don't think that boy will keep his mouth shut," Andra deduced. "And that if he tells people you had a woman in your room—"

"In my bed, no less!" said David.

"But I'm dressed."

"I doubt he noticed. And it'll get bigger and more untrue in the retelling."

Andra nodded; she knew this to be true. "Do you—?"

But then the crack in the door widened.

"Walter," David breathed in relief as his manager entered the room, taking care to close the door behind him.

He wasn't much by looks, was Walter; his white hair and dark-rimmed glasses, the fact that he was slightly shorter and heavier than average, had caused many people to underestimate his abilities. To their detriment. David knew there was no one better to have in his corner.

"Who's this now?" Walter asked, not unkindly, as his eyes settled on Andra.

"I have no idea," David said. "I mean, she says her name is…" He made a fluttering hand motion as the name escaped him, "and that I called her, but I didn't."

Walter peered at David. "How much wine did you have at dinner?"

"You know I almost never drink. Especially on set."

"Mm." Walter's gaze swung back to Andra. "So what are you doing here then, if David didn't invite you?"

"He did," countered Andra. "In a manner of speaking. But that's between me and him."

Walter eyed her for a stretch of seconds, and Andra had the idea this was supposed to intimidate her somehow. She merely stared back.

"Well," Walter finally said, looking again to his client, "throwing her out by force would only make for worse gossip. But it's up to you."

Walter always told David it was up to him. David knew better.

"Fine," said David. "Just keep Henry quiet."

Walter gave a short nod. "You're due in Makeup in less than an hour. Wait until everyone clears out for call, then slip her out of here."

David watched the door close behind his manager then turned his attention to the chifforobe that served as a closet for the room. Even though he would have to change in Wardrobe, David remained fastidious in his clothing choices; he found it was rather like armoring oneself. "You heard him," he said as he fished out neatly pressed trousers and button-up shirt. "Once everyone is out, you leave. Just make sure no one sees you coming from my room."

"And then what?" Andra asked.

David stopped himself just short of slamming the chifforobe door. "And then nothing. If I'm lucky, Henry knows the value of keeping his mouth shut."

"Not much of a scandal," mused Andra. "Might even make you more interesting."

"I can't afford to be interesting… yet. At least not in that way."

"You've thought this out," Andra said.

"Of course I have," David answered with a touch of exasperation. "Not everyone can just luck into this kind of work."

Andra nodded. "That's what I'm for. Usually. But you don't seem to need my brand of luck."

David hesitated. Standing there, with a fistful of clothes, it seemed impossible he was even having such a conversation with a strange woman who had turned up in his room overnight. But then again, given some of Alfred's stories, these things *did* happen. Show business was a circus tent of wonders.

Of course, Alfred was also a known liar. And nothing so very strange had ever happened to David. Until that morning.

Andra stayed still and quiet. She could almost see the debate going on behind the famous blue eyes. Well, almost famous. Very nearly. Or famous in certain circles, but soon to be… Whatever.

He was curious; they always were. But he was practical, too, which many of them weren't. He might go with his head over his heart.

And maybe that was the crux of the situation. It wouldn't be the first time. Although most of Andra's clients called to her for a career boost, she had used her gift to other purposes from time to time. Like that best-selling author who had been so lonely. Two days after meeting Andra, he met the woman he would marry. His second wife, but it was a successful union, and would continue to be until...

But Andra tried not to think about the balances.

Everything came with a price, after all. Everything in the world cost something, and people didn't always pay in cash.

And at that moment, David Styles was standing at the cosmic Cash Point. But would he make a withdrawal?

David glanced toward the bathroom. He should go get dressed, get moving. And Andra almost told him to do it, to go, to *run*. But she wasn't allowed to do that. She was only permitted to ask two questions: "What do you want?" and "Are you sure?"

Sometimes she didn't even need to ask the first one. The desire was so clear, so obvious, Andra could read it as if it were printed in Sharpie over the person's face. She always felt it was only fair, though, to ask the second question. She could ask it up to three times, though once was usually enough.

She couldn't warn.

She couldn't attempt to persuade or dissuade.

She could only ask her two questions and then do what she was there to do.

And sometimes it was fast, like with the author, and sometimes it took longer, like with the artist in San Francisco, but it always came to the same.

"What did you say you do?" David finally asked, and the words sounded drawn out almost as if against his will.

Curiosity had won.

Andra drew in a deep breath. "I'm a K<u>lêidouchos Propy-laia</u>. K-Pro for short."

"What is that, Greek?"

Andra was surprised. "Most people don't know that."

He gave a little shrug. "It's not popular to be too educated."

A smile tugged the corner of Andra's lips. "But you are," she guessed.

"I still don't know what it means."

"Translated it means 'holding the keys before the gate.'"

"You're a gatekeeper?"

"Sort of." She reached up and fingered the dual-strand silver necklace at her throat, well aware that, while David could see the topmost charm, the other was hidden beneath the neckline of her tank top.

He glanced at the bathroom again. "I have to—"

Andra nodded. Maybe he would escape after all. And would that be such a bad thing? Surely the flashes would stop either way. She had done her part, had come all the way to England to give him his chance, and that was what counted.

"Don't worry," she said when David continued to linger, "no one will see me leave."

"Don't go yet," he told her, and Andra suffered a moment of disappointment. He'd changed his mind; she would have to go through with it. But then he added, "Not everyone is out of the house."

She nodded again to show she understood, and David disappeared into the bathroom. Andra glanced down at the duffel bag she'd left beside the bed. Home again, home again, jiggity jig. She'd be gaining hours as she traveled, too; a bowl of gumbo and side of fried oysters for dinner was not out of the question.

Honestly, how long did it take a person to get dressed?

But Andra knew from experience that artistic and creative types came in two distinct flavors: those that threw on whatever they first found and never cared how they looked unless someone was dressing them, and those who spent their entire lives pretending they walked in a spotlight and that everyone was looking at them. Because deep down that was what they wanted. You could almost hear these kinds narrating their own lives inside their heads. They were the centers of their own stories, the stars of their imagined auto-biographical movies.

And the difference seemed to be just what David had suggested—those who lucked into their fame and fortune, or had it handed to them, versus those who had clawed their way in and worked for it. Because it was easy for the one type to take it all for granted, but the other kind of person *had* to look at himself as if from the outside; perception was every-thing, would make or break him.

Andra jumped at the sound of a door opening and turned expectantly toward the bathroom, so was doubly startled when a voice came from the other direction.

"Da—Oh, and who is this? David!" Alfred called without waiting for Andra to answer him, "Not like you to be hiding sweets in your room!"

Andra watched him slip into the room and ease the door shut behind him while keeping both hands behind his back, like a child that was trying not to touch when he desper-ately wanted to. She knew him, of course, had seen him in a few movies. Alfred Keenan usually played a charming troublemaker, both on screen and off if magazines were to be believed. His dark eyes ate up the sight of Andra sitting on David's bed, and she supposed this was the end of hoping for a clean getaway. Though it would say more about Alfred Keenan than David Styles if Alfred started gossiping.

"Or maybe it's very like him," Alfred said, lifting his eyebrows at Andra. She only stared back.

"Your name is Charlie?" he asked.

She shook her head.

"Your boyfriend's name is Charlie then? Father? Brother?"

Andra continued to stare at him blankly. It was like a strange sideshow, weirdly mesmerizing.

"I'm just looking at your necklace," Alfred finally explained.

Andra touched the charm again, the one hanging on the higher of the two thin silver strands that girded her throat. It was a small square striped blue, white, red, white, blue. A nautical signal flag. "It's just a C," she said.

"Well, it means Charlie, too," said Alfred. "And also…" He paused, his smile stretching just past pleasant. "Yes."

David stepped out of the bathroom then, neatly dressed and smelling of a soapy cologne. "Were you—?" He took in the way Alfred leaned against the door, closed his eyes and groaned.

"Never mind the act, David, who is she? I can't get a thing out of her," Alfred said, his eyes never leaving Andra.

Instead of answering the question, David asked one of his own. "Do you have a reason for being here, Alfred?"

"I do now."

"We'll be late for call."

Alfred shrugged. "So we'll be late. They can't get very far without us. Better yet, let's take her with us. Bet you'd like that, eh?" he asked Andra. "Hang around a movie set?"

"I've been on lots of movie sets," Andra told him flatly.

"Oh, a pro!" said Alfred with a laugh. "Which service did you use, Davey old boy? I want one like this one!"

"I didn't—It's not—"

Andra watched a flush start to creep up David's neck and wondered whether it was anger or embarrassment. Or both? Probably both.

"I'm just a friend," she said. "I forgot about the time difference and surprised him too early is all."

Again the dark eyes were on her, all over her, crawling like bugs looking for a crack to worm into. But Andra kept her gaze steady—she'd worked with enough men like Alfred not to be cowed by him—and he eventually switched his gaze to his co-star, whose own expression was remarkably blank.

"Well?" Alfred asked after a long moment. "Aren't you going to introduce me?"

"I know who you are, Mr. Keenan," Andra supplied.

Alfred finally came away from the door. "Alfred, please, call me Alfred. We're all friends here."

"Alfred, this is..." David began.

"Andra," she inserted when David came dangerously close to giving away that he'd forgotten her name. "Short for Cassandra." She tapped her pendant.

"Ah. Not Charlie," said Alfred.

"And not yes," Andra added.

Not liking the feeling of being left out, David attempted to move things along. "Well then, Alfred, we should..."

"You're not going to spend all day in here?" Alfred asked Andra in mock horror, handily sidestepping his co-star's attempts to usher him toward the door. "You must come down!"

"She's tired from her trip," said David.

"Worst thing you can do for jet lag is get off schedule," Alfred insisted. "Come, just for the morning. You can nap after lunch; it takes them ages to set up the lighting anyway."

Andra glanced at David, who was rather pointedly *not* looking at either her or his co-star. "I should shower," she said after a moment. "Maybe I'll wander down a little later."

"You look fresh as the proverbial daisy," Alfred protested. When Andra only stretched her smile thin, he sighed. "If you aren't down within the hour, I'll send someone looking," he warned, and Andra had the feeling he might not be entirely joking.

"Are we done?" David asked.

Alfred shrugged in a way that suggested he'd been

waiting on David all along, winked at Andra, and preceded David to the door, though he waited for David to open it for him. Andra had seen it all before, the myriad tiny ways two personalities negotiated their situations, doing this or that to promote oneself as superior in some way to the other. Many a client's deepest desire had surfaced as a sort of vengeance or comeuppance against a rival. Andra could not support these in the ways the clients wanted in that she could only affect change for the client him- or herself, never exert force over someone else on the client's behalf. There were ways to make it work—roundabout paths—but it meant going the long way, so to speak. And Andra never enjoyed it.

As she watched the door close behind David, she began to wonder if he would ask her to do something about Alfred Keenan. The idea depressed her, though she wasn't sure why. She'd had plenty of clients she didn't especially like or respect. Not the bulk of them, luckily; Andra did like most of those she was called on to help, and pitied a fair number, too. But she'd been so certain this one was unique somehow. Though, thinking about it as she dug fresh clothes from her duffel, Andra couldn't say how she had imagined it would be different. She'd seen it all before. She'd been training as a K-Pro since she was nine.

Andra started for the bathroom then checked herself and went to the door to the room instead and locked it against Alfred's hanging promise—or threat. The subsequent shower allowed her to relax a bit, and she even forgot where she was for a while. It was easy to pretend she was on a vacation when the client wasn't there, his interior lamentation acting as constant background noise.

That gave Andra pause as she was slipping on her sandals. She couldn't hear him, she realized; the weeping had ceased. And thinking back she came to the conclusion that it had stopped the moment he'd woken up and seen her.

This *was* different. No client had ever stopped wanting… whatever it was they wanted… just because Andra had turned up.

Something was really not right.

Andra looked again to her bag. She could just pack up and leave. If there was nothing more to be done—if the client had no deep-seated goal for her to guide him toward—there was no reason for her to stay. Case closed.

But Andra could practically hear her great-grandmother whispering in her ear. Leaving would be wrong. This person needed Andra's help, even if he didn't know that yet. She couldn't abandon him any more than she could abandon a child in the woods.

You get the call and you go. That was what Memam had always said.

In the meantime, Andra had no idea how she was going to pass herself off as an old friend of David's. It wasn't as if she could say they grew up together; her accent clearly proved otherwise.

She was just checking herself in the mirror, making sure her necklace was securely tucked under the sweep of her t-shirt, when the door handle turned. Jiggled. And then there was a knock, followed by the nervous tremor of Henry's voice. "I'm sorry, uh, Miss, er… Miss. But Mr. Keenan asked me to come check on you? Are you, uh… Oh!" he yelped as Andra pulled open the door. "Yes, you are."

"Mr. Keenan sent you."

Henry plastered a smile across his face. "Yes, well, he, um, yes. They're on set now, just getting, you know, dressed and, um, makeup."

He seemed ridiculously excited about the whole thing, and Andra asked not unkindly, "Is this your first job, Henry?"

His smile froze.

"Are you, what? Walter's grandson?"

And with that the smile melted entirely. "Grand-nephew. I'm not as young as I look," he added, momentarily forgetting to be deferential as defiance colored his cheeks.

"You should be pleased to look so young in an industry that prizes youth," Andra told him. "You wouldn't believe how many people I've worked with wish they could turn back the clock."

Henry began to lead her down the thick red carpet of the hallway and toward the stairs. "What is it you—?" Henry stopped himself from finishing his question, and Andra watched the confusion and worry play over his features; in his profession, putting a foot wrong could cost quite a lot. Andra was moved to put him at ease.

"I'm not an escort. I'm a K-Pro. No, you've never heard of it," she agreed before he could say it. "And if you're lucky, you'll never need one."

Henry nodded as if this made perfect sense and asked, "Did you want breakfast or anything?"

Andra couldn't help smiling; she supposed Henry was becoming used to strange remarks and requests and had learned early on to let many things slide. "You can just point me in the direction of craft services," she told him.

Henry hesitated on the threshold that would take them out to the patio and broad green lawns of the house. "I should take you to Mr. Keenan," he said. "But if there's something you'd like for breakfast, I can bring it to you."

And now Andra frowned. "It won't hurt him to wait a minute."

"He really doesn't like to wait."

"Doesn't much matter if he likes it," said Andra, stepping around Henry and into the sudden, heavy warmth of a summer morning. She hadn't realized how cold the house had been. She guessed it had to be costing a small fortune to keep the AC going in there.

Andra swung her head right, left, looking for the telltale signs of a movie set. All she saw was the empty patio and smooth green lawn that pushed down to overlook the water. But before Andra could come to any conclusions about the emptiness that stretched before her, Alfred came around the corner of the house, and seeing her, smiled broadly.

"There she is! Keeping her to yourself, eh, Henry?"

The young man colored instantly. "No! It's just—she wanted—"

"I was looking for craft services," Andra interjected.

"After all that, Davey didn't feed you," Alfred said, and Andra almost gagged on the overweening—and false—sympathy that drenched his tone. Then, sounding far less kind, Alfred said, "That's all, Henry."

Henry wasted no time in disappearing.

"Shall we?" Alfred asked, putting an arm out as if he expected Andra to step into his embrace.

She stepped away instead. "I don't understand this."

Alfred dropped his arm. "Don't understand what?"

"Your interest. In me."

"Any friend of David's," said Alfred with a negligent shrug, but the dark eyes remained bright and calculating.

"I don't get the feeling you and David are very good friends," said Andra. She went back to scanning the grounds. "Craft services?"

"It's all around the corner here," Alfred said, all business now. "Wardrobe and Makeup are inside where it's cooler, but we're doing outdoor scenes today, here, in front of the house."

Andra followed Alfred off the patio and around to the estate's looming façade. Having arrived in the dark, she'd failed to notice how impressive it was, and her face evidently showed her surprise as Alfred barked a laugh. "No, the

Internet photos don't do it justice, do they? Craft services truck this way." He led on.

They crossed the gravel-covered circular drive, passed the gathering of crew members setting up lights and sound equipment around what Andra took to be some kind of old-fashioned carriage, and struck off across yet more lawn until they came to what looked to Andra like the kind of food truck one found on the streets of New York or other large cities. Beside it was a long folding table covered in bowls of crackers, cups of fruit, plates of cubed cheese, bottles of water, and cans of soda. But Alfred ignored all this and went to the truck window.

"Mary? Are you in?"

A small, dark woman with frizzy hair appeared wielding a grease-smeared spatula. "You! What do you want?" She asked with mock severity.

"Not for me," said Alfred. "A friend."

"Since when do you have friends?" Mary asked as she turned to look at Andra. Froze. After a moment, she gestured at Alfred with the spatula and said, "I know what he is, but what in the hell are you?"

Andra's mouth fell open. This woman wasn't the first person to discern the difference in Andra—the fact that she had something else inside her, a power and abilities beyond the ordinary—but it had been a long time since anyone had. "I'm Andra," she answered, silently cursing the uncertainty in her voice. It almost sounded as if she were asking instead of telling.

"The hell you are," said Mary.

"Now, Mary," Alfred put in patiently, as if soothing an aging and befuddled parent, or perhaps an upset parakeet. "Andra would like some breakfast."

Mary eyed Andra for a moment longer before turning her

attention back to Alfred and waving her spatula at the bowls of snacks. "There's stuff on the table."

"Could you at least get her some..." Alfred turned to Andra. "What do you like? Eggs?"

"The table is fine," Andra said hastily. "Fruit. Fruit's good."

"I ain't catering, honey," Mary added.

"But you know you make better eggs than the catering company," Alfred said.

Mary snorted. "True. Fine. I'll make eggs." She disappeared into the truck again.

Andra opened her mouth to protest that, *no*, she really didn't need any eggs, but Alfred caught her eye and shook his head. So Andra stepped over to the table and popped open a lukewarm Diet Coke. "Where's David?"

"He doesn't eat breakfast," said Alfred. He paused, and Andra felt the prickle of his attention as it narrowed in on her like a laser. "As an old friend, I'm surprised you don't know that."

Andra nearly choked on the swallow she'd just taken. "We didn't usually wake up together," she managed, though her half gagging on her drink lessened the intended pointedness of her words. She surveyed Alfred, still dressed in the clothes he'd been wearing when he'd come to David's room earlier that morning. "Shouldn't you be in Wardrobe?"

"Should be," he agreed. "Hate sitting around in all those clothes in the heat, though, and it takes them forever to be ready to shoot."

"You'd rather have them wait on you than have to wait on them," Andra surmised.

She was rewarded with a flash of too-white teeth. "Smart girl."

Andra grimaced. Somehow a compliment from Alfred

Keenan didn't feel like a compliment at all. Quite the reverse, in fact. "Where is David then?" she asked again.

"In Makeup, like the good boy that he is."

"I'll go find him," Andra said.

"What about your eggs?" asked Alfred.

Andra was already taking rapid steps toward the house. "I didn't want any eggs."

"But you didn't eat anything else," Alfred called after her.

"I just remembered I don't eat breakfast either." Andra sped on, putting distance between herself and Alfred, Mary, eggs—all the things that felt like they could trap her, catch her in a lie that was beginning to take flight.

David remained still as Diane dabbed at his face, pausing periodically to cock her head in a critical fashion and examine the results of her efforts before leaning in again to continue. Like most everyone on the set, she knew better than to try talking to David; besides the fact that his moving his mouth might throw off Diane's work, his severe expression did not welcome chatter.

Indeed, David stared straight ahead, catching glimpses of himself in the mirror as Diane moved around him. He was thinking about his lines, the scenes; he'd left the day's sides up in his room (they'd been beside his phone) but didn't think he needed them, and there were always extra copies lying around anyway.

A change in the reflection as Diane stepped to his right caused David to start in his seat. Andra had slipped in through the doorway behind him, her long auburn hair swinging after her as she checked uncertainly over her shoulder.

Diane heaved a sigh patently designed to show David how inconvenient his motion had been and began swiping none too gently at his cheek with a makeup sponge. She spared a glance for Andra, who had stopped short inside the threshold. "Lost, dearie?" Diane asked without ceasing her attempts to make David's face camera ready.

"She's with me," said David and immediately wondered what had prompted him to say it. As he met Andra's own surprised eyes in the mirror, he felt a stab as if an arrow had been shot through his core. The sensation was so tangible David glanced down to check his chest, only to have Diane jerk his chin upright. This time, however, David made it a point to avoid Andra's return gaze in the glass, focusing instead on the glint of the charm at her neck and working arduously not to allow his eyes to travel any lower down the V of her t-shirt.

Diane gave David's cheek a final daub. "That's about done." She drew off the nylon drape and tissue paper collar designed to protect David's wardrobe from her machinations, and suddenly David felt unmasked. Which, he was quick to remind himself, was ridiculous; there was nothing of David Styles in the gray cutaway coat, the bright blue ascot, gold waistcoat or striped trousers. It was all character. Mr. Hastings. He sat forward in his chair and admired the shiny shoes, continuing to avoid Andra's unstinting and inquiring scrutiny.

"Let me get your hat," said Diane, disappearing before either David or Andra could respond.

"It's a period piece," David explained, though he still didn't raise his head. Diane returned with the top hat, and David reached for it, but she held it away, and only after he lowered his arm did she situate the hat on his head. "Don't touch it," she told him once she had it adjusted to her satisfaction. And so David, self-conscious in the way of someone learning to walk while balancing a book on his head, eased to the edge of the makeup chair and then stood and slowly turned as if to present himself to his audience of one, even as he mentally armed against any derision she might choose to throw at him. Actors couldn't afford thin skin.

Except when he finally did get facing the right way, hat still neatly poised, Andra was no longer there.

INSTEAD OF THE relief he might have expected, David found himself somewhat deflated. It wasn't so much *her*, or so he told himself, as the fact that no one likes, when thinking they are in company, to discover they are in fact alone. David was sure he would have felt the same had it been Alfred who had wordlessly defected. But then, no, there were times when being alone was preferable.

David murmured his thanks to Diane and, pulling Mr. Hastings' known sense of confidence around him, marched for the door, only to come up short against Alfred. Or tall, rather, as David had a good four inches on his co-star and the top hat only served to increase his height.

"Don't you look natty," Alfred said, but his dark eyes were darting around the room already, bright with interest, like a magpie looking for something shiny to collect.

"You just missed her," David told him.

Alfred's shoulders relaxed, and his expression sharpened into something nearing solemn. The look sent a pang through David; he had never seen Alfred look so serious except for a camera.

"There's something strange about her, don't you think?" Alfred asked.

David wanted to say, *Of course there's something strange about her, she turned up out of nowhere and keeps asking me what I want.* But since Andra was supposed to be an old friend, such an answer didn't seem very diplomatic. So David said, "Not a very nice thing to say about one of my friends. Anyway, I thought you liked her."

Alfred's eyes met David's, and for a long moment they simply stood there. It occurred to David that he should probably step aside and allow Alfred into the room—Alfred was the senior star here—but Alfred also didn't appear to be in any particular hurry. His eyes ran over David as if reading his face, his posture, his thoughts. David remained still for as long as he could stand to, but finally impatience, and perhaps a little anger, a little fear, prompted him to open his mouth, only to have anything he might have tried to say cut off by Diane.

"Alfred Keenan, you get in here. Should have been done ages ago."

And with that, it all collapsed. Alfred's face seemed to jump like a DVD skipping a scene, and all at once he was his usual, affable self. He shot David a rueful smile and slipped past, saying, "Where's Tina?"

"Got tired of waiting for you. Stuck with me now," said Diane.

David didn't stay to hear whatever witty retort Alfred came up with. He stepped out into the main entrance hall of the house, a grand space of marble and brass and polished wood that David hardly saw as he aimed for the daylight sailing through the open front doors. Today's scenes were arrivals and departures, departures being first because they took place in the morning. If Alfred kept them waiting much longer, he'd have Mac breathing fire down his neck for wasting daylight.

A period piece, no matter how popular the book had been, had not been at the top of David's list of dream roles. But besides the very good cast that had been assembled, it had been the chance to work with Mac that had sealed the deal. Benjamin MacKenzie was one of the best known and most highly respected directors in the business; he had his pick of projects, and if he wanted to make something, it got made. David could only dream of ever having that kind of clout.

Now, as he stepped out of the portico and into the morning sunlight, David spotted Mac slouched to one side in his chair and smoking a cigarette as he watched the animal handlers, who in turn were watching the crew hitch the horses to the carriage. "Where the fuck is Alfred?" Mac called as he spied David. "We're going to end up with a glare."

Opting not to shout, David strolled over. "He's in Makeup."

"For Christ's sake," Mac hissed, "go—Holy shit, is that Andra?" Mac sat up in his chair, dropped the cigarette to the grass.

"Um, yes?" David answered uncertainly as he discreetly set his heel over the still smoldering butt. It was summer, after all, and the weather had been dry.

Mac turned the full force of his gaze up at David. "Andra Martineau? You know her?"

"…Yes?" David said again. He began to glance around, unsure of where Andra had appeared.

Mac cupped his hands around his mouth—he was famous in his refusal to use a bullhorn—and yelled, "Andra!"

All motion on the set paused for a full ten seconds as crew members looked to one another in search of the direc- tor's target. Then, having determined they were not it, they began work once more.

David followed the direction of Mac's shout and saw Andra was playing ball with a frisky black Labrador; was that part of the film or had someone brought their pet along to the set? But Mac's shout had drawn Andra's attention, and she was looking at them now as the dog danced around her legs, dropping the ball, waiting, then picking it up again, trying to coax Andra into another toss. She didn't seem to notice, her face a blank, though even at that distance David was able to see the brilliant, catlike green of her eyes, their color emphasized by the sunlight slanting across them. They were like something out of a science fiction movie, David thought, the kind of thing you wore a special suit to keep from being exposed to. Radioactive. That was the word. But even as he was ruminating, even as it crossed his mind that Andra's eyes hadn't seemed so acidic in the makeup mirror, David watched as she turned back to the Lab to give it a final scratch behind the ear, and by the time she directed her steps toward him and Mac, the yellow in her eyes had filtered away, leaving them a more natural, seafoam color.

"What—?" But David stopped there. Because now he wasn't sure whether he'd imagined the difference, whether it had been a trick of the sunlight.

Mac chuckled and rose as Andra approached. He wasn't much taller than her, and David towered over them both; for the first time since leaving school he had the desire to slouch or at least sit. He blamed the hat.

Mac flung open his arms, and Andra obediently stepped in for a hug, quick kisses on each cheek, before moving back again, though David noticed Mac kept his hands on Andra's arms. "What brings you back to me?"

David half expected Andra to look at him, indicate him somehow, but she only smiled in a Mona Lisa way and said, "The shaggy Lennon look is working for you."

The Mac David knew would never have let anyone side-step him so easily, but the director merely slipped an arm around Andra's waist and turned toward David, though his eyes remained clamped to the woman beside him. "I met Andra… God, how long has it been? It was just before *Dream of the Jade Dragon*. You told me not to make that one. I should have listened."

"It didn't hurt you any in the long run," Andra said.

"But after that blew up it took ages to get anyone to agree to let me make *House Afire*. How is it you know David Styles?"

If there was something accusatory or suggestive in the director's tone, Andra ignored it as she turned the full wattage of her gaze on David. He took an involuntary step back as he fancied gold streaks shooting across the green of her irises like so many tiny shooting stars. Good God, what was wrong with him today?

"We're old friends," was Andra's reply.

Mac smiled at David in a way that was not entirely amiable. "She's a good friend to have. You could do a lot worse than to have someone like Andra in your corner."

"He seems to be doing well enough on his own from everything I've read," said Andra.

"Read a lot, have you?" David asked sharply. He didn't entirely understand the conversation happening around him, and he didn't like being the subject of it either. And for some reason he especially didn't like the way Mac's arm tightened around Andra as if she were something precious David might steal. "Maybe I should go see how Alfred is coming along."

"You do that," Mac agreed, and as David walked away he heard, "Andra, you don't have to go yet, do you? Come sit here next to me."

Craig will love that, thought David. Craig was the assistant director (which didn't count for much when Mac was the director since Mac kept tight control of his set and was reluctant to ever hand the reins to anyone else) and took his job very seriously. And because his job consisted, in large part, of sitting in the chair next to Mac's, Craig was sure to be about as pleased as the papa bear in a fairy tale to find it occupied by someone else.

Well, it's not my problem, David reasoned as he entered the house's great hall and made his way back to Makeup. Diane was laughing at something Alfred said as she placed his top hat over Alfred's ridiculously springy hair. Even Diane's liberal application of oils and gels couldn't tame Alfred's dark curls.

Diane sobered when she caught sight of David, and for the first time in his career, David realized what he considered his professional demeanor might actually work against him in some circles. It came in a flash, so quick and so clear, that David drew back as if he'd been slapped.

Noticing the change in Diane's attitude, Alfred turned in the chair and lifted an eyebrow. "They've called in the dogs, have they? Or dog, rather. Just the one."

"Andra is out having a nice chat with Mac," David offered as a temptation. "Evidently they're old friends."

Alfred's brows came down. "I thought *you* were old friends."

David only shrugged.

"Curiouser and curiouser," said Alfred almost leaping from his seat, hat wobbling. He stopped long enough to give Diane a peck on the cheek. "Thanks, love. And give this one to Tina for me," he added, landing a second smooch on the other side.

"She won't take it from *me*," Diane told him.

"Then keep it as a spare and tell her I'll pay my tab with interest later," Alfred called back to her, his voice bouncing off the walls and ceilings of the house's entrance as he preceded David back to the set, faster than David had ever seen him move. If David's legs hadn't been twice as long as Alfred's, David supposed he might actually have had to hurry to keep up.

"You're shagging Tina?" David asked, with the idea of being conversational as proof that he was actually friendly, even as he tried to remember which one was Tina.

"I have a reputation to maintain," Alfred replied. "It's

never a bad idea to go with one of the girls in Makeup if you can; then they have an interest in keeping you pretty. Ah!" Alfred stopped just outside the doors but remained in the shade of the portico, using a few of Mac's precious minutes to observe the way the director leaned into Andra to speak to her, the way Craig hovered behind her, then took in David's own stern features and said with something that might have been satisfaction, "Aren't we just getting to be a cozy crew?"

4

Craig Vauderhagan had spent his early years engrossed in movies in the way that only a pudgy, freckle-faced redhead boy with no friends to speak of can. More than just a passive observer when it came to the matinee shows at the corner cinema, Craig had learned all he could about the very processes involved in each of his favorite films: casting, location scouting, the directors' choices, pre-production, post-production, studio involvement, distribution deals, sets, storyboards, last-minute changes to scripts, creative differences... Craig had packed every ounce of the information he was able to obtain into his not unintelligent grey matter and, when it had failed to impress his classmates (and, later, anybody else who wasn't in an online chat room at one in the morning), he'd used it to get into film school, on to an internship, and finally a job. But not just any job. No, as Craig often reminded himself when feeling a bit down about the fact that girls still didn't find all the trivia he knew attractive: *he was assistant director to Benjamin MacKenzie*. Wait until his old schoolmates read *that* in a magazine.

He was taller now, but still freckled and ginger and slightly too round. And even "taller" was relative; full grown, Craig Vauderhagan stood only five foot eight. On days when he was suffering from doubts about his abilities, Craig wondered whether Mac had only chosen him because Mac himself was short but Craig was still shorter.

That morning, however, Craig was in good spirits. He loved a nice outdoor shoot in fine weather. And he was pleased that he'd been able to wrangle a room in the house instead of being sent to stay in one of the hotels. It was a tiny room, almost an afterthought, and a hotel bed would almost certainly have been more comfortable (plus a hotel would have had a television), but it was better than nothing. Mac needed Craig to be readily available to talk about each day's work; Craig staying in a hotel would have been inconvenient for everyone involved.

At least, that was how Craig chose to look at it. Because, really, Mac had given him almost nothing to do and didn't even seem to know Craig was staying in the house. In fact, in the back of Craig's mind was the worry that, if Mac did find out, he'd send Craig to stay in one of the hotels after all.

It was this little raincloud of a thought that, coupled with the discovery of a strange woman in his chair, put Craig's day on a downhill slide.

Under normal circumstances, Craig would simply have ousted the outsider from his seat; he was the AD, and he could do that, even to attractive young ladies that were likely as tall as he was. But the circumstances were clearly not normal, judging from the way Mac leaned in close to talk earnestly to this woman to the exclusion of all else around him. Mac was known for being restless, for having his hand in everything, his eyes everywhere at once. But just then the director's eyes were in only one place, his typical facile form of conversation replaced with something plainly more mean-ingful and significant.

Given this evidence, Craig opted to approach with caution, though he did so with a certain amount of speed as well because for one thing he knew they were already behind on filming for the morning (damn Alfred Keenan, who said he was five eleven but was in all probability not more than five ten-and-a-half), and for another he was intensely curious about what was going on. Was it possible the woman was from the studio? Who else would Mac take so seriously? But then why not take her into the house and talk in private?

A few feet from the chair, Craig slowed his pace. Striving to appear nonchalant—but also busy, because Craig believed looking busy contributed to the general notion that he was important—he strolled up to where Mac and the visitor sat and came to a stop behind his chair. Mac didn't turn, but the woman did. She blinked up at Craig, her eyes large and clear, the color of pale green jade. "Is this your chair?" she asked.

"Never mind," said Mac before Craig could answer, "he can stand for a minute. Now this other project I'm thinking about…"

Craig started to lean in, but just then someone tapped him on the shoulder, and he turned to find the gaffer—Johnny, who Craig knew had worked most recently on *The Passion Fields* starring Norman Elders and with Ben Jakkobs directing (Craig couldn't seem to help dialing up minutiae every time he encountered someone)—towering over him. Craig opened his mouth, intending to say something smart and authoritative, but Johnny merely nodded his head toward the house. Following the gesture with his eyes, Craig spotted Alfred and David stepping out from the shade of the portico.

Craig looked to Mac, but the director had taken no notice of the arrival of his tardy stars. Sensing a chance, Craig seized it by calling, "Rehearsal's up!" He looked again to Mac with a smile that was meant to say, *See there! I did something useful!* Alas, unbeknownst to Craig, he mostly resembled a happy, if overweight, Irish Setter waiting hopefully for a treat.

Mac had stopped talking to Andra to frown up at Craig for a moment before turning his attention to the set. Alfred and David had stopped short when Craig had called for rehearsals; Liz, always on time and thus always waiting, was ready by the carriage, along with the handful of other actors involved in the scene: Tamara, Mark, Lydia, a couple others whose names Mac could never remember because they were all unknowns and the parts were so small. Mac called them whatever he liked, and they answered to it, never bothering to correct him, which meant he might never know their actual names until he reviewed the list of credits. If part of him felt bad about that, another, stronger part of him felt these people should have the courage to speak up and the wherewithal to make him remember who they were.

Now Mac glanced up at the sun that was swiftly rising over the trees of the house's east lawn and shouted, "God-damn it, Alfred, you'd better show me you're worth what we're paying you! We don't have time for more than a couple of walkthroughs at the most if we're going to avoid the glare. Can you do it in two?"

Aware that all eyes had swung to him, Alfred made a show of laughing off Mac's ire. "*I* can. But David may need more than that."

Mac waved this off. "David's an actor; you're a star. That's how I know David will do what he's told. It's you I have to worry about."

At that, Alfred dropped all pretenses and strode toward the carriage. "Let's do this then."

Still standing behind the chair he felt he should have been sitting in, Craig straightened in anticipation. Mac gave him the nod, and Craig called again, "Rehearsal's up! Quiet on the set!"

"Put 'em through their paces, would you, Craig?" Despite Mac's phrasing, it was more a command than a question. "Andra and I need to finish our conversation. Let me know when they're good to go."

Craig squared his shoulders, feeling taller than ever. Never mind the chair; he didn't need it. Everything was rolling his way now, and Craig was determined this would be just the beginning.

"DAVID," Alfred drawled, "care to join us?"

Glancing around, David realized the others had returned to their starting marks. He grimaced and stepped back. He was having difficulty remaining focused. He knew the lines, recited them as automatically as a person singing along to a well-known tune while driving, his mind elsewhere all the while. Between takes, and despite trying not to, his eyes darted to where Andra continued to sit beside Mac. David was terribly aware of her watching him, but it was her blank expression that bothered him, though he wasn't sure why; he only knew he wanted her to at least appear interested. Which was strange considering he'd started the day wanting her to be anything but.

"She *is* just an old friend?" Alfred queried from his left.

David's gaze flew again to Mac and Andra. Just a friend, yes. No! Not even that. *God in Heaven*, thought David, *don't start believing your own story.*

The clapboard sounded and the scene began again.

"WHAT'S WRONG WITH DAVID?" Mac was wondering aloud.

From where he stood monitoring the video assist, Craig came alert. "Sir?"

"I wasn't asking you," Mac told him. He turned expectantly to Andra, "You're old friends, right? Anything going on with him?"

Andra shifted uncomfortably against the canvas on which she sat. "Well," She drew the word out in an attempt to buy herself time to think. "You know, I came out to see him because…" And here she let the words hang; she didn't have anything more to say.

Of course, Mac filled in the open air with his own assumptions. And if Craig was paying attention to what was being said—or not being said—neither Andra nor Mac noticed.

Whatever conclusion Mac reached, he didn't voice it, only sighed. Then, cupping his hands around his mouth, he shouted, "David! Wake up and focus! Mr. Hastings is an energetic character, and you're playing him like a narcoleptic!"

David looked over, nodded his understanding, stepped back to his mark. And while Andra detected a fair amount of determination in his face, she saw traces of the forlorn as well.

"Let me talk to him," she said, slipping out of the chair.

"Hey!" Craig called after her, then realized his seat was finally free. He hurried to reclaim it while Mac's attention remained on the woman crossing the set to where the actors stood waiting for cue.

"Andra, darling, has Mac added you to the cast?" Alfred asked as she stopped short in front of David.

"Who's this?" Liz asked.

"Old friend of David's. And Mac's, too, apparently." Alfred's lips stretched like a snake uncoiling as he looked to their visitor. "You just know all kinds of interesting people, don't you?"

She ignored him. "What do you want?" she asked David, alarmed at the desperate tone she heard in her own voice.

David only blinked, a small frown on his face.

"Just tell me or let me go," Andra pleaded.

But David's brow furrowed as he shook his head. He felt as if he had static between his ears. "I don't…"

"Shouldn't we finish this shot?" asked Liz.

"Yes, David," said Alfred, "tell her you want to finish this scene so we can get in out of the heat."

"Would it help you concentrate if I weren't here?" Andra asked.

Unable now to think at all with her standing there, those green eyes on him making him dizzy and nauseous, David started to bring his hands to his face, was startled when something prevented them from getting there. A bolt ran through him as he realized Andra had taken his hands in hers.

"Your makeup," she said by way of explanation. Froze. Something was wrong. Andra heard it like a rolling thunder, going so far as to turn her eyes briefly to the empty summer sky in search of signs of an unexpected storm.

But of course there was nothing. The sky was a clear, blank expanse of blue.

So Andra looked again at David, whose dark blue eyes were digging into her in a way that made her distinctly uncomfortable.

Wait. *Dark* blue? If there was one thing everyone knew about David Styles, it was that his eyes were a bright, light blue. The color of a Caribbean sea. Or the Mediterranean, depending on which magazine you read. In any case, not this strange slate color.

Meaning to let go of David's hands, Andra started to draw back and away, but he closed his fingers and held on.

"I want my key back, Katie."

For Andra, the words were like a crack of lighting split-ting the world in two, complete with the high-pitched howling of a wickedly cold wind. Her breath stopped in her chest and she rocked on her feet; the only thing that kept her from falling outright was David's unrelenting grip.

"That's not the line," Liz said, and the spell was broken. Andra used the moment to pull her hands free, and at the loss of her touch David blinked like a man waking from a dream. All at once he had a blazing headache. He reached again for his face but stopped himself short of touching it, eyeing Andra all the while.

For her part, Andra watched David's eyes clear, the dark-ness parting from them like rainclouds breaking open to allow daylight to shine through. And somewhere in the back of her mind, the screaming stopped again. "Alfred's right," she said when she realized everyone was still staring at her, "It's hot out here. I'm going…" She didn't finish the sentence, merely beat a hasty retreat.

"WHERE'S SHE GOING?" Mac asked as he watched Andra all but run for the house.

If he hadn't been so happy to have his chair back, Craig might have noticed the ominous tone in the director's voice. As it was, Craig only shrugged.

Mac rose. "Get the shot," he instructed as he headed inside.

Oh yes, Craig's day was definitely looking up.

INTERSTICE

She knows her way, even in the nigh total dark of a
moonless night. She slips nimbly between the tombs,
past the mausolea and stele, many of them as tall and
taller than she.

Behind her she hears him, but he is not so familiar with
this ground; this is her sacred space. She can hope to put
more distance between them, if not lose him entirely. Having
to dodge the funerary monuments will at the very least slow
him down. Even as she listens for him, stretches her ears to
catch the telltale of his breathing or the slap of his footsteps,
the sounds are growing fainter.

And still she nearly stops.

She nearly turns around.

He will think she only ever loved him for the key. Or
worse, that she never loved him at all, that she made a play
of it, a game, an act. He will think the key was her goal all
along.

But if she were to turn around and explain…

Her steps slow. She is coming near the edge of the cemetery, will soon be back on the path and unsheltered from

view. Should she stay in the shadows of the tombs? Should she go back to him and try to justify her actions? He might let her keep the key if only he understood her need for it.

But she knows the key is his most prized possession. And they have argued over it before. There is no reasoning with him.

A footstep sounds somewhere to her right, and Hecate stills her body and her breath and waits. But there is no other noise.

He is close. So close. She feels it in every part of her; his body calls to hers in silent song, making her yearn to go to him.

But she steels herself. Tightens her grip on the key. And turns to run once more.

5

Katie... Katie... But no, not Katie. 'Cate. They sounded nearly the same, and both were nicknames, the first for Katherine, the second for...

Hecate.

But how had David known? No one used that old name any more, that old aspect of the Greek goddess from which Andra—and her ancestors before her—derived her work and power.

Andra folded herself onto one of the lowest of the entry's sweeping stairs and clasped her hands around her knees; she was sweating in spite of the hard-blowing AC.

David *hadn't* known, of course. *Didn't* know. But something inside him did, and *that* was the thing that had called her to England, the thing that had quieted once she'd come within reach.

So what was it and what did it want?

Well, she knew what it wanted, didn't she? The key.

One of Andra's hands began to drift toward her neck, only to fall as Mac burst through the doors.

"Are you all right?" he demanded without preamble.

"I'm fine. It's just the heat."

Mac dropped down beside her and frowned. "Don't give me that. You're from New Orleans; heat has never bothered you." When Andra didn't respond, Mac pushed on. "Did David do something to you?"

"No," said Andra, and in her own ears her voice was too loud, too sharp.

"Was it Alfred?" Mac asked.

Andra shook her head. "No, I think I'm just tired from the trip over." She considered faking a yawn but decided Mac had worked with enough good actors to know a bad one.

Mac opened his mouth to keep pressing, but the doors flew open again, revealing the round silhouette of AD Vauderhagen. "I got it!" he crowed.

"Got what?" Mac snapped, standing.

Craig practically skipped over to the staircase. "I got the shot, just like you said."

"Fine. Good. Tell them to break for lunch."

"I already did." Craig's gaze slipped to where Andra still sat; he hoped she was from the studio and taking note that Benjamin MacKenzie had asked him—Craig Vauderhagan—to take over on set, something Mac never, ever did. Not only that, but Craig had sailed through with colors flying, even if he did only say so himself.

Mac saw the way Craig's gaze lingered on Andra and scowled. "Anything else?"

Craig jumped. "Uh, no, I guess not. I'll just..." He backpedaled for the doors.

"Craig," Mac called, and the assistant director halted. "If you want to keep that chair of yours, I suggest you find something for Miss Martineau here to sit in."

"Right," said Craig. "Absolutely. Will do." He made good on his exit, running the name Martineau through the files of his brain, and giving Alfred a wide berth as the actor stepped into the entry.

"What do you want, Alfred?" Mac barked, and Alfred paused, though only for show, before continuing his leisurely progress across the waxed and polished wood to where Andra sat and the director stood.

"To get out of the sun, mostly," said Alfred, removing his hat and dangling it as he leaned over the stair railing. "Though I'm not convinced Craigy Boy really got as good a shot as he thinks he did. Something appears to be very wrong with David," Alfred added, dark eyes sliding to Andra.

Andra met the gaze steadily, forcing down the soupy turmoil that swirled in her stomach.

"You should go to lunch," Mac told his actor.

Alfred kept his eyes on Andra. "And you must be hungry, too, seeing that you didn't have breakfast." When Andra only continued to stare, Alfred heaved a sigh meant to showcase his much-tried patience. "We could dine al fresco on the patio. There's a good breeze on that side of the house." And when she still did not respond, he added the enticement, "David will be there."

"Go on, Alfred," Mac broke in testily. "We'll be along in a minute."

But Andra was rising. "I *am* hungry," she said.

Alfred smiled, lifted his eyebrows at the director and tapped his hat back over his curls. "You wouldn't dream of keeping her from her lunch, I'm sure."

Mac watched as Andra took the couple steps down. "You're okay?"

"It's David I'm worried about," Andra admitted.

"I'll take care of him," said Mac.

Alfred offered an arm, and Andra took it without thinking though her attention remained on the director. "It's not his career that concerns me," she said.

"Me either," Mac confirmed.

Alfred tugged gently with his elbow, inducing Andra to move forward like a horse on a lead. "We'll eat first," he insisted. He threw another smile at Mac. "We wouldn't want to keep anyone waiting for the afternoon shoot simply because we were late for lunch."

Mac snorted. "Go."

"You're not coming?" Andra asked.

Mac waved her off. "I've at least got to check what Craig canned. I'll be there in a bit." He stalked toward the main doors while Alfred led Andra through the house toward the patio and side lawn.

"No use going back outside if we don't have to," Alfred said.

It was then that Andra realized she was holding Alfred's arm. She started to withdraw her hand but Alfred covered hers with his other and gave it a pat.

"He's really not well?" Andra asked. She braced herself for some kind of cutting response, something meant to be funny and cruel, but Alfred surprised her.

"No," he said as they neared the threshold to the patio, and as Andra glanced up she caught his grimace, "he's really not." Alfred paused in front of the French doors and pulled his arm nearer his body, drawing Andra in with it so that she stood close and kept. It occurred to Andra then that though Alfred Keenan was not an especially big man, he was a strong one.

"Why did he call you Katie?" Alfred asked.

Andra attempted to extract herself without appearing obvious or afraid, but Alfred remained unmovable. "I don't... I mean, he didn't."

The dark eyes scanned her face as if reading something written on it. "He did, and you know why," he concluded, even as he released her and reached to open the door. A gust of heat entered the house, borne on the wings of the breeze off the water; Andra could smell the damp, and the humidity hanging heavy in the air was so like home that for a piercing moment she was heartsick for the bayou.

"If he's having some kind of breakdown, I deserve to know," Alfred continued, breaking into Andra's thoughts. "I won't jeopardize my work for a weak co-star, and David never struck me as one able to deal with the kind of attention fame is likely to bring him."

"Charming," Andra remarked dryly.

"Charming is not the same as kind. And kind sometimes has to give way to practicality. As much fun as it would be to see David in the tabloids, I'd rather he did it on some other set than mine."

Andra had the idea that Alfred Keenan wasn't the type of man to be kind in any case, no matter how charming or practical. Head high, she stepped out the door and onto the patio, and Alfred followed to where industrious crew members had erected an open-sided tent, the canvas popping whenever the breeze gave an extra push, to shade the long lunch table where the actors had congregated. It was there David sat, silently pushing his fork at a mass of salad while Liz burbled alternately at him and, failing to draw David out, the woman on her other side who, from what Andra could tell, was dressed as some kind of old-fashioned maid.

The chair on David's right was vacant save for David having set his hat there, but in any case Andra thought it best to keep a little distance and so took the seat across from him instead. Liz stopped talking then, and the table grew quiet. Andra scanned the dubious faces around her, stopping at David's, but he only continued to prod lettuce around his plate and hadn't seemed to notice anything around him had changed.

Andra was starting to think maybe she should just leave

when a plate of chicken with a side of some kind of fried rice mixed with vegetables landed in front of her. Alfred took the chair on her left and set his own plate down. "What are we all talking about?" he asked.

David looked up and grimaced before going back to arranging his cherry tomatoes.

Andra eyed the chicken. It smelled really good, and she realized she hadn't eaten since the flight. And that had been airline food.

Liz finally spoke up. "We're wondering if Craig really thinks that take was any good."

David went still but didn't look up. Andra understood that what wasn't being said—or, at least, what David assumed was not being said but was meant anyway—was *he* was the reason the morning's filming hadn't gone well.

"Well, he had to do something," said Alfred as he sliced his chicken breast. "The light was going to be all wrong before long. Poor thing, running to daddy Mac to show him what a good picture he'd just drawn."

Around them, the conversation began to spill free once more as everyone swapped stories of run-ins with Craig. "I swear he was trying to look down my dress," one woman declared, only to have another snicker, "That'd be some trick considering you have a good three inches on him in those boots."

Once Andra was sure she was no longer of interest to anyone, she began to eat, only to realize a moment later she *was* of interest—to Alfred. He'd set down his cutlery and was leaning his head on his fist, watching her. Andra froze, fork poised over the piece of chicken she'd just cut.

"C for Katie?" Alfred asked.

Across the table, David's fork clattered as he dropped it, dinging first against the wood of the table then, a moment after, the hard stone of the patio.

Alfred didn't even look over, his eyes fixed on Andra. "If you spelled it with a C, of course."

"I already told you it's for Cassandra," said Andra. She watched as Liz reached down and retrieved David's fork, stopping to wipe it clean with a napkin before handing it back to him. David accepted it, though his expression suggested he wasn't entirely sure what the fork was or what he was expected to do with it.

"But you go by Andra," Alfred persisted. "Why wear a C and not an A?"

Exasperation rose in Andra like the surging of a tsunami, but she fought it down; in her experience, people like Alfred counted it a victory if you showed any kind of temper—they liked getting the better of those around them. So Andra made it a point to set her fork down gently instead of throwing it and declared, "I think I'll take a look at the garden."

"In this heat?" Alfred asked.

David set his fork down as well and rose from the table. "I'll come with you." When the conversation around them faltered, he added, "We have so much to catch up on after all these years."

Andra was not unaware of Alfred's gaze as she and David walked down the steps to the lawn; the dark eyes were hotter on her back than the midday sunshine.

ACROSS THE WIDE green at the side of the house was a garden, in full bloom in early June. Andra and David walked toward it in silence, side by side, though Andra noticed David was careful not to walk near enough to even accidentally brush or touch her. The closer they came to the colorful jumble of plants, the stronger the smell of them became, the breeze off the ocean below only managing to blow around the hot air and heavy perfume of flowers.

"It's just a bay," David said, unprompted, just for something to say. "An inlet, really."

Andra nodded as if this were an interesting and important fact.

"You see how the land gives way," David gestured to the far side of the garden, which was bordered by a short wall of piled stones. It didn't look to Andra like it would stop anyone from falling; on the contrary, Andra thought someone might be just as likely to trip on it and go flying out into the open air.

As if reading the direction of her thoughts, David said, "It's not that long a way down."

There had been no path on the lawn, and there wasn't one in the garden, either, only grass between the flowerbeds, though the landscapers had left plenty of space. Andra guessed four people could walk shoulder to shoulder between the plantings. Or, in their case, it was just enough room for her and David to maintain a comfortable distance from one another. Now they meandered past hot pink something-things (Andra was terrible at gardening, though she could identify roses and tulips pretty definitely), and yellow other things, and some whites and purples, steadily making their way toward the wall.

"Something there is that doesn't love a wall," Andra quoted.

"What?" asked David, sounding yet again as if he'd only just arrived from somewhere else. Andra wondered where he went when inside his mind.

"Robert Frost," she said. "The poet?" When David only continued to stare blankly, Andra added, "You probably don't have to learn him over here."

"We've got plenty of our own," said David as he picked his way through some yellows that lined the wall, presumably planted there to keep people away from it, though

David's long legs allowed him to get over them with relative ease. He took a seat on the uneven pile, and Andra blanched as one of the flat, smooth stones shifted beneath him.

"What's wrong?" David asked.

"That's not really very safe, is it?"

David glanced over his shoulder. "It's fine. It doesn't drop straight to the water, you see? Kind of like a ha-ha. But without the cows."

Andra didn't know what a ha-ha was, or what cows had to do with anything, nor could she see what David meant from where she stood, and she didn't want to. Something panicky fluttered in her chest. "The stones are loose," she pointed out. "They're just piled, not, you know, stuck together or anything."

David cocked his bright eyes at her, and in that moment Andra saw just why they were the subject of so much Internet fan-girl chatter. The brilliant sunlight only served to make them clearer, so that they rivaled the sky for color. All at once Andra felt like she were falling forward and found herself thankful she wasn't anywhere near the open drop. Reflexively, she dug the heels of her sandals into the grass as if to ground herself, and David's eyes traveled away from Andra's face to her feet, restoring her to rational thinking.

"You should sit," said David, "if your feet are bothering you."

"They're not..." Andra began, but there was no good way to explain what had just happened. "Anyway, you shouldn't be sitting there. Look, you're stepping all over the whatever-they-ares."

"Am I?" David leaned a little forward to look past his own knees while simultaneously lifting his feet, and the rocks beneath him teetered.

A fresh wellspring of panic bubbled inside Andra.

"Please," she said, no longer caring that she sounded whiny and childish.

"Narcissi," David mused.

Stung by what she thought was an insult, Andra retorted, "Fine, go ahead and fall if you're going to be that way about it."

David lifted his head—too quickly, as it turned out, the momentum of his movement causing the rocks he was perched on to finally give way. They slipped out from under him like a deck of cards fanning and sliding, and David fell backward, head and shoulders first in an ungraceful somersault.

Without stopping to think, Andra lunged forward and was just able to grab David's ankles before he went full over. *He's got big feet,* she thought haphazardly as David's left shoe fell into the dirt. *Smelly, too. Sweaty socks.*

"You can let go."

Andra didn't. But she did crane forward to see over the wall.

David had been right about there not being a direct drop to the water. In fact, the land past the wall sloped gently downward to meet the bay, grass eventually giving way to a mixture of scrub and pebbly sand. The wall, then, acted as something of an optical illusion to make the house appear higher and grander than it actually was.

David, meanwhile, rested in a rather undignified pose, legs up and hooked over what remained of his spot on the wall, and ankles firmly held by Andra so that he couldn't quite sit up all the way. He propped himself as best he could with his palms on the uneven ground. "It really would be easier for me to get up if you'd give me my feet."

Andra released him and bent to retrieve his lost shoe. David accepted the no longer very shiny loafer, dropped it to the ground and stepped into it, then moved to step back over the wall.

"Don't you know what a narcissus is?" David asked.

Andra felt a chill move through her, and goose pimples appeared on her arms despite the warmth of the day. "Rings a bell."

"I wandered lonely as a cloud?" David pressed in exasperation, and Andra found herself glancing uncertainly into his eyes, but they were as bright blue as ever.

"Daffodils. Wordsworth," said Andra automatically, even as something in the back of her mind tried to rear itself out of the mire of old fairy tales and myths. The image of a boy leaning over the stillness of water flashed across her memory, quick as a fish, gone before she could fully catch hold of it.

"At least they teach you something over there," said David. "Like poetry, do you?" When Andra threw him a questioning look, he gave a halting explanation. "We're supposed to be old friends. Seems like something a friend might know."

"What should I know about you then?" Andra asked. "Besides what I've read in magazines?"

She was surprised when his cheeks turned pink with something more than a sun-induced flush. He stepped past her and back onto the grassy path of the garden, giving Andra no choice but to follow. "I don't know. What have you read?"

"That you're tall and have blue eyes."

He glanced at her, swiftly, and Andra saw he thought she was making fun of him. She'd worked with so many self-assured, over-confident personalities she forgot they could sometimes have soft underbellies. "Well, and that your mother keeps pet peacocks," she added, dredging up a random fact from one of the articles she'd read.

He looked at her then. "They wrote about Mum?" he asked, and Andra was forced back a step by the mixture of outrage and anxiety in his expression. Were his eyes darkening again?

But before Andra could hazard an answer to either David's question or her own, Alfred appeared, David's top hat in hand. "We're due back," he said as he handed the hat to his co-star. "And by the look of it, you'll need some touching up."

Andra's eyes swept over David, trying to see him objectively, and concluded Alfred was right. The sun and heat hadn't been good for David's makeup, the breeze hadn't been good for his hair, and the fall had been nigh disastrous for his clothes.

Andra looked over her shoulder, back at where the garden wall was now broken, leaving a slice of the ocean visible. "We should find someone to rebuild the wall."

"Elves?" Alfred suggested with an arched eyebrow, and Andra couldn't keep her mouth from falling open in surprise.

David glanced between the two of them and, not trusting whatever seemed to be passing unspoken there, began to walk ahead, saying, "Let's not keep everyone waiting."

THEY MADE it halfway across the lawn, Andra and Alfred only just able to keep pace with David's long strides, before David, muttering words of excuse and apology, disengaged himself to speed farther ahead. He'd had a bad enough morning, and he wasn't especially looking forward to the fuss he knew would be coming from Makeup and Wardrobe. Indeed, Rachel the Wardrobe Mistress showed her singular displeasure at the state of David's jacket by raising her eyebrows, compressing her lips, and not saying a word as she stripped it off him and set aside to clean and mend. She went and fetched another, as well as new trousers and shoes, and David was obliged to change right there, while Rachel watched with arms crossed, as if she thought he might ruin *this* suit just by putting it on.

It wasn't unusual, of course, for actors to need some fixing up between takes and after breaks. But the very extent of the fixing David required—paired with the lively gossip circulating about his "breakdown" that morning—placed him in the status of being both popular (as a topic) and unpopular (as the source of so much extra work). It was something David felt keenly as it radiated off those with which he came in contact, first Rachel and next Diane as she quickly and fiercely tidied his face and hair: a burning curiosity mixed with utter disapproval.

David could not afford to let these few incidents color everyone's perception of him. He'd worked too long and too hard to get where he was to allow such a deathblow. And the more he thought about it while sitting in the makeup chair, the angrier he became.

Because this was, of course, all Andra's fault.

It had started that morning, with her turning up in his room. And things had only gotten worse as the day had gone on.

By the time Diane had given his top hat a final brushing, David was well and truly determined to have Andra off the set and out of his life for good.

ALFRED DREW Andra up short as David stalked off across the lawn. "Poor David," he mused. "Not his day, is it?"

Andra pulled her arm free of Alfred's and took a couple steps backward to put more space between them. She rubbed unconsciously at the spot near her inner elbow where they'd been touching, as if to wash the contact away.

Alfred regarded her for a moment, shoved his hands into his trouser pockets and began walking again. Andra stood there a second longer before trailing after him toward the set.

"If I didn't know better," said Alfred, his voice carrying back to Andra, "I'd think it was you."

This stopped Andra in her tracks. She'd only ever been good luck to the people she'd been called on to help, opening the doors to their dreams. It had never even occurred to her the opposite could be true. Her? Bad luck? That just wasn't how it worked.

Aware that he'd lost his companion, Alfred stopped and turned. Waited. But Andra only continued to stand there, planted. With a sigh, Alfred began to make his way back to her.

"I said I knew better," he told her, taking her arm once more.

"You don't know anything about it," said Andra.

"Care to explain it? No?" asked Alfred as Andra's lips became a thin and obstinate line. "Well, I do know that if I don't get you back to Mac soon, he will make not only me suffer, but everyone else besides. You wouldn't want to be responsible for that, would you?"

He had her there. Andra felt bad enough about David not to want to extend her guilty conscience to his cast-mates. So she allowed Alfred to lead her back to the set, all the way to the now three folding canvas chairs, one of which was occupied by Mac while Craig hovered behind the other two, clearly torn between his desire to sit beside the director and the knowledge that the middle chair was meant for Andra.

"Maybe you should sit in the middle?" Craig suggested to Mac. "Better sight line."

Mac frowned up at his AD, ready to snap, but the sight of Andra arriving on Alfred's arm mercifully distracted him.

"Here she is," Alfred announced, handing Andra into the chair reserved for her. "Fed and walked."

"Alfred," Mac warned.

"Only joking," Alfred put in smoothly. He looked to Andra, "No offense taken, I hope?"

Andra shook her head dumbly, her mind too busy swirling over Alfred's earlier suggestion that she might in fact be bad luck rather than good to voice an answer. It wasn't possible, was it?

"Go have Makeup fix your hair," Mac instructed Alfred and, after executing a dramatic bow for Andra's benefit, Alfred strolled away.

"I hope he wasn't too insufferable," Mac said to Andra. When she only shook her head again, he asked, "Are you all right?"

"I think maybe the jet lag…"

"But Alfred's been behaving? And David? I meant to talk to him," Mac added, eyes scanning the set for the tallest of his stars.

"Don't," Andra said, too quickly, and Mac's frown landed on her. She struggled to explain. "You'll only fluster him more, and then the afternoon won't go any better than this morning did. Better to wait. I think he's pulled himself together."

"He better have," Mac muttered. "Where is he?"

Had it been a cue, Mac couldn't have argued with the timing; David chose that moment to step out the doors and, without a glance in Mac's and Andra's direction, moved to join Liz and the handful of other waiting cast members. Andra watched as Liz tentatively attempted conversation and was rewarded with David's full attention and what appeared to be coherent replies.

Something in Andra's stomach contracted like a cramp,

and all at once she felt the need to leave. But as she stood, Mac asked, "Where are you going?"

Andra looked down at the director and tried to recall him as she'd once known him some years before: young, enthusiastic, energetic. Benjamin MacKenzie had always had vision, had always been capable; he'd just needed a boost into the right spheres. Andra had done that for him, and the consequences of Mac's success had thus far remained well-hidden scars: insomnia, nicotine addiction, a paranoid streak, and the lack of sustainable romantic relationships common to a certain strain of Hollywood types. Worse was coming—Andra felt it like vibrations in a spider's web—but that wasn't her concern. Mac wasn't at all her concern any longer, and so without bothering to answer his question, she began to walk away, back toward the house, toward her duffel bag, the first steps toward going home.

But behind her Mac asked, "Is it David?"

Andra halted. Damn Mac's shrewdness.

"I can get rid of him," Mac went on.

Andra turned around then, incredulous at the suggestion and Mac's off-handed tone. "You're in the middle of filming."

Mac shrugged. "It's only been a week."

"Your schedule…"

"It wouldn't be the first time a film lost an actor early on," said Mac. "Better early than later."

"You would do that?" Andra asked, her voice rising with increasing astonishment. Members of the set began to glance her way.

"If he bothers you…"

"Just because he bothered me? He doesn't," Andra added swiftly as Alfred's suggestion that she might be bad luck for David flashed through her mind; the last thing she wanted was to get him fired. "David and I are—"

Mac saved her from having to speak the lie by finishing

for her, "Old friends, I know. But even old friends can fall out. What brought you here to see him, exactly? Did he call you?"

"Kind of," Andra answered weakly but was rescued from having to elaborate by the ever-efficient Craig.

"Rehearsal's up!" the AD called as Alfred wandered out of the house, appearing to be in no particular hurry. Alfred stopped just outside the doors, not going to the trouble to join his fellows, instead only watching as Liz laughed at something David said, earning a half smile from David in return. At which point Alfred swung his gaze to where Andra stood, looking, she knew, for a reaction. But Andra was determined not to give him the satisfaction; she gritted her teeth against the strange seizure in her chest caused by Liz's attention to David (and vice versa) and chalked the nausea up to not having eaten enough.

"They're not listening to me," Craig said, a thread of disbelief running through his voice.

Mac heaved the world-weary sigh of a man surrounded by those he considered less competent. "Rehearsal's up, people!" he shouted, and the actors obediently moved to their marks, Alfred throwing a tiny shrug at Andra before falling in with the others.

"Come sit," Mac said to Andra.

"I shouldn't. I wouldn't want to be a distraction."

"If he's worth his salt, he won't let anything distract him," said Mac, and his tone set Andra on edge. It was fair to guess Mac now had David in his sights, and that it was Andra's fault David was *persona non grata* with his director, meaning (in Andra's mind), she had to at least try and mend the fences broken on her behalf. So with a mixture of resignation and determination, she resumed her seat. She wouldn't be bad luck; she refused to be.

She watched everyone but David, looked everywhere but at him, even when he was speaking, though the timbre of his voice continued to cause a shortness of breath in her. Instead, she worked at listening, striving to hear whatever was inside David, to figure out what it could be. This thing that had literally caused the light in David's eyes to go out, this thing that knew Andra held the power of Hecate...What did it want? She asked the question—the one she'd been trained to ask—silently, and strained to hear the answer. But there was nothing. It was utterly quiet.

Was it waiting for something?

It had demanded the key, had said it wanted *its* key back. But the key was hers, had been passed down through the family for ages. Andra wished she'd asked Memam more questions about its origins. Maybe knowing more could have helped her find a solution to the problem.

Andra was so engrossed in her thoughts, she was surprised when Mac called, "That's a wrap!" She looked up to see the actors simultaneously slump like puppets whose pull strings had been released.

Turning in the chair beside her, Mac tossed down his cigarette butt and asked, "Dinner?"

HE'D REMEMBERED, Andra discovered, that she liked crispy fish tacos with avocado and a spicy rémoulade. Not a terribly common dish, even on the English coast where fresh fish was easy enough to come by, but Mac had either found someone who could make it or had bullied the catering company into doing it on the fly.

He'd had someone set up a cozy table on the balcony of his room, too, bistro-style, although he'd mercifully left off any attempt at romantic candlelight. Instead, Andra and Mac were in prime position to watch the sun set artistic blaze to the tops of some tall evergreens, turning them from green to black as it sank behind their gathered masses. Candles,

Andra figured, would have been overkill. And as a director with a keen sense for visuals, Mac surely knew this. Just as he'd planned enough in advance to have this all done and ready long before asking Andra to have dinner with him.

Andra had accepted the invitation with a mixture of relief —she hadn't especially wanted to spend a meal crossing swords with the overly curious Alfred, nor had she relished the idea of watching Liz steadily working to improve David's humor—and apprehension. Mac had led her straight off the set and into the house, and Andra had made it a point not to look back. Up the stairs and through the labyrinthine halls... Andra wasn't sure what she'd expected, but she'd balked when Mac had thrown open the door to what was obviously his room.

"If I eat with them," Mac had explained as he entered the room, "it's no fun for any of us. They don't feel free to talk, and you know me. I might just lecture. So I usually eat up here." He'd gestured at the tall windows to the far right of the room. Andra had stayed in the doorway, unconvinced entering the room was not somehow like signing a waiver or agreeing to a tacit contract of some kind, but leaning to look she'd seen that the windows went all the way to the floor and so served doubly as doors.

"Fish tacos, right?" Mac had asked.

And Andra's stomach had growled a hearty reply.

They'd spent the meal talking about various of Mac's projects because Andra felt it was unprofessional of her to discuss her clients in any detail. While her occupation certainly had no written code of ethics, no oath or standard privacy privileges, much of what Andra did was so personal she chose not to talk about it except in the broadest anecdotes.

"Enough about me," Mac said once the plates were empty. He refilled Andra's wine glass and then his own before sitting back in his chair with his usual sloppy posture. "Bet you never thought you'd hear me say that!" he added with a laugh.

Andra smiled. "It's fine." And it *was* fine, more than fine, because Mac's chatter had taken the pressure off her. On the whole in her experience, those working in entertainment were generally happy to talk at length about themselves and their work with only minimal prompting.

"But what about you? Where have you been?"

Andra shrugged. "Here. There. Around."

"And now you're here. To see David."

Ah, there it is, thought Andra. Once she'd left a client, she seldom saw them again, though she received frequent letters and e-mails and an impressive number of holiday cards. Of course she'd run into previous clients once in a while, but Andra worked to keep her time with them brief lest things become awkward. Andra knew too much about the people she'd worked with, saw into them too easily for either her comfort or theirs. It had never occurred to her, then, that one might become jealous of her attentions to another. Even if Mac didn't know her real reasons for coming to see David, his antennae were clearly up, searching for a signal.

"I thought he might need me," Andra hedged. "But I think I might be making it worse instead of better."

"Making what worse?" When Andra only stared at him over the rim of her glass, Mac said, "Look, if one of my actors is having problems, I need to know. I can't have him disrupting the whole shoot."

"You sound like Alfred," said Andra.

"Jesus, I hope not." It was said with a half smile, but Andra couldn't help noticing the calculating glint in Mac's eyes; he was, she knew, trying to put the puzzle together. "Tell me how you know David," he said.

Andra evaded. "Haven't seen him in ages. But I don't think he wants me here anyway."

"I want you here," Mac told her. "I always did like having you around." When again Andra was silent, he added, "I've had them make you up a room. Here, I'll show it to you."

Mac pushed back his chair and stood, and Andra followed suit. They cut through Mac's room and out into the hall; as they passed doors, Andra wondered how she would ever remember which room was hers. After three turns (Andra had counted), Mac stopped in front of a door, opened it, and stood back to allow Andra inside.

It was a beautiful room, but then all the rooms Andra had seen at the estate had been beautiful. This one featured an Aubusson rug in cream, sage, and mauve, with swaths of the original hardwood left uncovered. There was a large fireplace surrounded in carved marble, an ornate writing desk trimmed in gilt, and a bed with posts tall and sharp enough to be dangerous.

"You like it?" Mac asked eagerly, and again Andra wondered at his enthusiasm for her, his devotion and desire to please. So far as she knew, Mac didn't normally work to please anyone but himself.

"I hope you didn't have to displace anybody," was all Andra could think to say, standing in the center of the splendor.

"Nobody important," said Mac. He turned to go, taking hold of the doorknob but then hesitating. "Do think about it."

"Think about what?" Andra asked.

"Staying. We finish up here in four days. You can at least stay that long."

The same queasy feeling that had clinched Andra's stomach and chest on set earlier did so again now; she couldn't imagine staying, not even four days, watching David while whatever was inside him watched her. Surely she should put some distance between herself and it? And if she *was* bad luck for David in some way, far better to step aside, out of the picture. He'd be better off without her hanging around. Unless, of course, her leaving resulted in his being fired from the movie. Or the thing inside him damaged him in some way. So for David's sake as much as Mac's Andra gave a little nod. "I'll think about it."

"Good. And good night." Mac pulled the door closed behind him.

Andra stood there a little longer, unsure what to do next as her mind swirled with all the pros and cons of staying versus leaving. Feeling a headache coming on, she ventured to look at the bathroom, which was much bigger than David's had been, with China blue walls and dainty porcelain fixtures. There were packets of paracetamol in the cabinet. Andra took some and was just considering a shower when she realized her bag was still in David's room. The thought gave her pause. Could she make do without her bag for the night? Maybe go for it after call the next morning? But no, Mac had said over dinner that call the next day would be later, and Andra thought she'd be more likely to stumble upon David in his room if she waited until morning than if she went right away. Hoping he might be lingering over dinner, Andra ventured out of her room to go in search.

7

Unable to take any more of Liz's giggling and pawing or Alfred's smirking, David had retired early, only to find himself unable to sleep. He'd taken his ritual shower, turned out the lights, and gone to lie down, his mind an unceasing drift. That cursed Andra mucking up his life, and how was she friends with Mac anyway? The mental image of Mac tightening his hold on Andra's waist popped up behind David's eyelids, making it impossible for him to close his eyes. He rolled onto his side and saw the dent in the pillow beside his, the place where Andra's head had been that morning. For God's sake, weren't the maids supposed to fix that? And yet he couldn't quite bring himself to smooth the indentation. So after tossing and turning a while longer, David switched on the bedside lamp with the idea of distracting himself by reading something... Except, he discovered, there was nothing in the room to read.

David liked to read, made it a point to travel with a book in hand for long flights or train trips, but somewhere between having wrapped the television miniseries he'd just finished and coming out to the estate for this project, he had finished one book and failed to pick up another. He had all but ransacked his room in search of a magazine, a copy of the script, *anything*, when his eyes landed on a purple duffel beside the bed. Not his bag. Andra's.

David hesitated. He didn't like to think of himself as the kind of person who would pry into a near stranger's things, and really, he knew he should probably make sure Andra's belongings were returned to her. Besides, even if she did happen to have a book in there, David wagered it wasn't likely to be anything he would be interested in reading.

But something would be better than nothing.

And a quick look wouldn't hurt anyone.

David bent down and unzipped the bag then proceeded to poke questingly through the tumbled mass of clothing, drawing his hand back sharply when he identified something lacy as an undergarment of some kind. He was ready to give up when, crowded amid some toiletries, he caught a glimpse of the kind of discolored and bent pages one associated with a much-read paperback. Like an archaeologist working not to disturb a final resting place, David reached in and neatly withdrew the one artifact that interested him. He hadn't even had a chance to look at the title when someone tapped on the door. After throwing on his robe, David opened the door to find Andra on the threshold, her head bowed so that most of what he saw was the top of her head.

"I just came for my bag," she said, her voice so low David had to bend forward slightly to catch the words. He got a whiff of something flowery—her shampoo or perfume—and only just stopped himself leaning in closer as he reminded himself sternly how inconvenient her being there was to begin with. Another little flare of anger at the way she'd turned his world over was lit within him.

"You're leaving?" he asked, and if he sounded hopeful, he didn't care.

She lifted her head then, big green eyes blinking. "Not tonight. I just need my bag."

Scowling, David stepped back to allow her into the room. "I suppose you'll go stay at the hotel."

But Andra didn't move; she was staring at the book David was holding. "Is that mine?"

"Um..." David took the opportunity to look at it. "Michael Crichton? Really?"

"You went through my things?" Andra asked.

"I was just looking for something to read."

"In my bag?" Andra pushed past David and swept across the room to where her bag still lay, unzipped and open. "What else did you pry into?"

"Look, you come here, and you give me the worst day of my life, nearly ruin my career in one blow, and then give me more trouble when all I want to do is borrow a blasted book!" He tossed the paperback so that it tumbled over the bed, stopping just short of falling off the other side where Andra stood. "Take it and go away, for God's sake!"

Andra didn't touch the book. She zipped the duffel, swung it onto her shoulder, and stalked toward the door. But before Andra could reach for the knob, the gap she'd left when she'd entered widened to reveal Alfred, his dark eyes sparking with interest.

"I thought I heard a fuss. Old friends already tired of one another's company?" Alfred asked. His eyes traveled to the bag over Andra's shoulder. "Don't say you're leaving us already!"

"She'll be more comfortable at the hotel," David said flatly.

Andra shot him a glare. "I'm not going to the hotel."

David stiffened. "You said—"

"I never said. You assumed." Turning to Alfred, Andra's tone sweetened considerably. "Mac found me a room here in the house. If I can find it again."

"And how long do you plan to stay?" David demanded.

Andra rounded on him again. "What difference could it possibly make to you?"

"I only like to know how close to me my bad luck is living," said David.

He'd struck a nerve; he saw it in the way she flinched, and in how quickly she turned her face away. Scoring such a verbal win gave David the same feeling as when he knew they'd nailed a scene, that it was perfect, except instead of exhilaration or relief David felt like a hole had opened inside him. He felt hollow.

Alfred went so far as to flash David a black look, and that was saying something because Alfred had a famously high threshold for rude behavior. Slipping an arm around Andra's waist—an arm, David noted with a glower, she did not resist —Alfred said to her, "Let's leave David to his temper tantrum, shall we? And I'll help you find your way back to your room. Do you remember which way the windows faced?"

"I don't know," Andra said as Alfred guided her toward the door. "It was a few hallways down from Mac's room."

"You were in Mac's room?" Alfred asked Andra as he followed her into the hall. From over his shoulder Alfred shot David another look, but David was at a loss to interpret this one. Whatever Andra's answer, David didn't hear it; Alfred pulled the door shut decisively behind him, leaving David with only Andra's discarded paperback for company.

. . .

"It's where he eats his dinner," Andra said.

"Not usually," Alfred replied.

Andra was so surprised she stopped walking. "But he said..."

"Well, you *are* old friends, aren't you? Had some catching up to do, I suppose."

Andra didn't especially like the smile Alfred offered her. And he made it sound as if "catching up" were something indecent.

"I am sorry about David, though," Alfred went on, gently herding Andra back into forward motion. "Not sure what's got into him." Though again, to Andra it sounded as if Alfred knew exactly what had got into his co-star, and the insinuation was far from pleasant.

Andra knew *something* had got into David all right, though she didn't know yet exactly what it might be. And her ideas about the nature of what was inside David were likely far different from anything Alfred had in mind.

"How did the two of you meet?" Alfred asked as he continued to steer her through the halls.

Andra evaded the question by remarking, "I think I turned here before."

Alfred obligingly ushered her around the corner. "You've known each other a long time?"

"Not really," Andra admitted. "In the scheme of things, I mean. I've known Mac longer."

"And I can see Mac would like to lay prior claim," said Alfred. They came to the end of the hall, which formed a T with another corridor. "Which way?"

"I don't know. God, why don't the rooms have numbers?"

"Now what old estate house puts numbers on its doors?" Alfred chided. "It would be far too tacky. Mac's room is down there," he added, pointing left.

"Then I'm probably down there," said Andra, pointing right.

"Right it is," Alfred said, and they marched on.

"Oh, here!" Andra said after they'd passed another couple doors. "I'm pretty sure…"

"Better knock to be safe," Alfred suggested, and he gave the door a firm rap. When no answer came, he turned the knob. "Look familiar?"

Andra leaned in to look. The rug, the big bed. "This is it." She stepped in and Alfred followed, though he didn't move past the threshold.

"Interesting. This was Liz's room. Wonder where he's put her."

Andra's throat tightened. She couldn't afford to make more enemies on the set and could only imagine what kind of reaction the starlet might have at being displaced. "But Mac told me he hadn't relocated anyone important."

"Depends on his definition of important, doesn't it?" Alfred pointed out. "It's all relative. Liz clearly isn't as important as you. In Mac's book, anyway. But look, you've got a balcony." Alfred's smile didn't go as far as his eyes, which were hard like pebbles. "David will be jealous."

"I'll trade with her," said Andra, hating how distressed she sounded but unable to help it. "She can have the room back. I don't need anything this big."

Alfred shrugged. "I doubt she'd take it back now. Ego, you know." Then he winked. "But I'm sure she'd be happy to take your spot in David's bed if you don't want it."

Andra felt everything inside her freeze; she had temporarily forgotten Alfred was not, in fact, her friend, and now she felt as though she'd been bitten by a snake hidden amid flowers. "It's not mine to give," Andra said, struggling to keep her tone even.

Alfred only shrugged again and turned back toward the

hallway. "No need to worry about sleeping too late; call isn't until eleven."

"It's not—" Andra began, but Alfred was already gone. After a moment she dropped her bag and went to close the door, then locked it for good measure.

INTERSTICE

He curses the tombs and the moonless dark—he cannot see. Nor can he hear her; she is too light on her feet, too at home in the dead hours, for this is her time and she gains strength from it, whereas his power comes with the dawn.

The night is cold and so is she; how is it he never realized until now? She has no feeling for him, for any of her divine kin. All her trips down from Olympus... Why could she not stay home and settle? Why must she insist on roaming? And now she needs his key, she says, to help these humans. Why not stay above where it is quiet and leave the people to their own devices?

It is an ancient tradition of the gods to meddle in the affairs of the world. But if their pleas really bother her as much as she professes, she could just as easily shut them out. He does it all the time. The prayers and invocations are only so much background noise... Though he does enjoy the occasional animal sacrifice.

He is so busy thinking, he nearly stumbles over a stone that has fallen from one of the monuments. The mortal body he inhabits when on Earth is clumsy and bothersome; he cannot understand how she willingly takes on such a frame. But he stifles his frustration. Leans against the nearest tomb and stops to listen. He cannot hear her, but he can *feel* her. Off to his left. His heart gives a tiny, silent cry, and he senses that she is primed to answer; an invisible thread is pulled taut between them.

And then she is gone again.

He sighs. Mother had warned him Trivia—Hecate—would never do for him. Just once, he would have liked Mother to be wrong.

He straightens, ready to begin the pursuit once more, and as he does so he hears it, distinct in the crisp, still air of night: the gates of Olympus slamming shut.

8

I f there was any bright side to sleeping in what Craig assumed was some kind of converted storage closet (besides, of course, the joy and luxury of staying in the house at all), it was that the room, being in a nestled part of the house, was very quiet. Or it *had* been, anyway, until that night.

Craig had been lying on his bed reading the latest issue of *Empire* when he noticed a sort of squeaky, hiccoughing sound coming from... Where exactly? Craig sat up to listen.

The sound was somewhat regular, and at first Craig thought it must be some bit of machinery in the house, a dishwasher maybe. (He wasn't sure, but based on the smells that came through the vents, he thought he was near the kitchen.) But as the sound began to taper off and Craig started to settle back into the lumpy mattress, a fresh spate of hiccoughs began, and Craig realized that, no, it was not the sound of a dishwasher changing cycles. Someone was sobbing.

Of course, Craig reasoned, the best thing to do would be

to ignore it. Crying people usually didn't like to be bothered. And Craig would not want to add to anyone's burdens.

But then again, if there were somebody down there... perhaps another crew member... Or what if someone was lost? The woman from the studio? As AD, Craig felt it was his responsibility to make sure all was well.

Also, the bed was really uncomfortable.

Craig got up and shuffled to his door, opened it a crack. He was in a part of the house that had never been meant for family members; the halls and rooms in his quarter were the province of the staff, and this fact was reflected in the narrowness of the corridors, the plainness of the décor with its worn carpeting and dark paneling, and the miserliness of the sconce lights, which were too dim and spaced slightly too far apart to be entirely useful. And so, looking out the crack in his door, Craig couldn't see much of anything. But he could hear the weeping more clearly, though it seemed to be abating. It was coming from somewhere on his left.

A new idea seized Craig. What if the house was haunted?

He shook this notion off almost as quickly as it had come; if the house were haunted, he would have read about it on the Internet. And he'd been there a week without seeing or hearing anything until that night. No one else had mentioned anything, either, and they definitely would have; nothing like a good ghost story on set. No, this was something—someone —real.

Craig pushed his door open wider, cringing a little at the shrill whine the hinges made in protest. His neighbor had heard it, he was sure, and as if to prove it, the sobbing stopped abruptly.

Craig hesitated, unsure whether to push on or just go back to his bed.

But the bed really *was* uncomfortable.

Craig stepped out into the mostly dark hallway; it smelled

of dust and the kind of heat generated by too much heavy equipment (a smell with which, as a film worker, he was especially familiar). For a fleeting moment Craig wondered whether he should worry about potential electrical fires. But then another stray hiccough drew his attention to the door on his left.

He'd never assumed it was another bedroom. In the week they'd been at the estate, Craig had never seen or heard anyone else down there aside from the occasional house staff sweeping past in the hall. He wasn't even 100% sure they came to clean his room regularly because, having been raised by the kind of mother who expected such things, Craig was in the habit of making his own bed and hanging up his towels after using them.

Now Craig reluctantly dragged his feet toward the door in question, all the while reminding himself that being successful in his line of work sometimes (often) meant doing things he didn't like or want to do. Including knocking on strangers' doors and attempting to console them when they were keeping him from reading a magazine. Mac had once said, if not to Craig directly then at least while he'd been within earshot, "The director is like a father figure on the set." Of course, Mac had been talking about the need for strict discipline after an unruly group of actors started a row in a pub, but if the director's job was to be a father, Craig conjectured, then the AD could just as easily act as mother.

With this idea lodged firmly in his brain, Craig squared his shoulders and knocked on the door.

"Go away."

Craig's shoulders fell. The voice was muffled but almost certainly female, which made things all the worse because Craig, not terribly at ease with his own gender, was much less so with the opposite.

"Are you all right?" Craig asked through the door. "I

could..." What did women like when they were sad? "Get you some tea?"

There was silence. Then suddenly the door swung open, and Craig found himself blinking at Elizabeth Hellmann, the closest thing their ensemble cast had to a leading lady. She looked decidedly different without her elaborate blond wig, makeup, and period clothing; her brown pageboy, freckles, and jeans made her appear petite and boyish. And without her shoes, she was actually shorter than Craig.

"What are you doing down here?" Craig asked. He was so surprised he forgot to be delicate and motherly.

"Did he send you to apologize?" Liz demanded. "Well, you can tell him—"

"Who?"

"He didn't send you?" asked Liz.

"My room is next door," Craig told her. "I heard... What are you doing down here?" he asked again. He was starting to wonder whether he'd fallen asleep and was dreaming.

Liz made a strangled sort of noise that Craig associated with angry cats and spun away from the door, marching back to her bed and flinging herself facedown onto it. Craig stood there a moment, had just decided he might be better off retreating altogether, when Liz sat up and announced, "He gave that Katie bitch my room."

"What—?" But before he finished the question, he knew the answer. The studio woman, of course.

"Oh, he's promised we'll find me a better room tomorrow," Liz went on, "but as for tonight..." She swept her arm at the space, which was almost exactly like Craig's, right down to the quaint duvet that had been made to look original to the house. At least, Craig liked to think it was only *made* to look that way.

"Tell me," Liz insisted, "do you really think this is the best they could do?"

"At least it's quiet," Craig offered. "And better to be here than the hotel."

"He should have put me in Lydia's room and sent her down here," said Liz. "I mean, I don't know who this friend of his is, but..."

"She's with the studio," Craig said, his hypothesis pole-vaulting into fact despite his inability thus far to find Martineau in any of the directories.

Liz stared. "You're kidding."

"Who else does Mac go to so much trouble for?"

"No one," Liz conceded. "But I thought they were just old friends?"

Craig bit his lip against admitting he didn't know for sure. "They've definitely worked together before. He's constantly pitching projects to her."

"And she seems to know David, too," said Liz. She began to chew thoughtfully on her thumb. "Who *is* she?"

Again hoping to avoid having to confess his ignorance, Craig asked, "Do you want me to see about getting you another room?"

But Liz only stood up and waved his offer aside. "I have other plans." She stood up, slipped on a pair of canvas shoes with no laces that had been tucked under the bed, and started for the door, Craig still standing in its open frame; he rocketed backward when he realized she was ready to go straight through him. But once Liz got into the hallway, she stopped. "Which way?" she asked.

"To where?" Craig countered.

"Back up to where the real rooms are."

Mutely, Craig pointed left in the direction of the stairs that led to the main floor of the house. He would have explained that she would need to switch staircases to get all the way up to the "real" guest rooms, but Liz was gone before he could open his mouth.

.   .   .

DAVID LAY down on the bed and gave the book a kick to send it off the far edge; he was determined not to read it, no matter how bad his insomnia. Which, as it turned out, wasn't that bad, as he dozed off with the bedside lamp still on. He fell almost immediately into a dream of someplace dark, the blackness tangible like smoke, as he pushed through it in search of something. Or someone. He wasn't sure who or what he was looking for, but he felt he'd almost reached the point of catching up to it when he was startled awake by a new pounding on his door. A sensation of frustration mingled with regret as David opened his eyes and forced himself to sit up.

It occurred to David a lot had changed in twenty-four hours. His room, which he preferred to think of as a haven, had become Victoria Station. All starting with that damnable Andra. Was she back for her book then? As he swung his legs over the edge of the bed, he caught sight of the paperback and scooped it up, then went for the robe he'd flung over the back of the vanity chair. After several half-asleep, failed attempts, David realized he couldn't hold the book and put the robe on at the same time, and in exasperation flung the book onto the bed.

As he finally got his robe sorted, the knocking became more furious. "A minute," David said though his voice, thick with recent sleep, wasn't loud enough to be heard over the rapping. David pulled open the door to save it from any more abuse and was surprised to find Liz there, though he knew he really shouldn't be. What surprised David more, however, was the tiny stab of disappointment he felt when he saw his co-star. Andra hadn't come for her book after all.

"Yes?" he asked, disappointment and fatigue preventing him from being as polite as he might normally be. Without the elaborate wig and dress, the heavy makeup, and the heeled boots that made her a good three inches taller, Liz took on more of a "kid sister" appearance. Her bob cut, freckles and plimsolls lent her a sporty and almost childish air. But her next move dispelled the notion. As David began to ask what she wanted, Liz reached up to draw his face down for a very un-sisterly kiss.

There was a moment, brief as a flashbulb, in which David asked himself when the last time was he'd kissed anyone outside of a stage direction. And there was another moment, only slightly longer, in which he attempted to remind himself that getting involved with co-stars was on his personal list of prohibitions, but his brain stopped working before he could complete the thought.

He was ready to buckle when Liz broke it off. "Can I stay here tonight?"

"What?" David asked stupidly. He was aware of having lost his bearings; the world rocked around him like an uneasy ocean.

Liz pushed him back out of the doorway and into the room, allowing herself in and closing the door behind her. "Mac gave your friend Katie my room," she explained.

"What?" Oxygen was returning to David's brain, and with it his sense. Katie? Who was Katie? And yet for some reason the name sent a chilly arrow through him. He tightened the belt on his robe, as much against that as against any further assault from Liz.

"Who is she, anyway?" Liz asked. "This old friend who knows you and Mac from way back when? Craig says she's with the studio. Is that how you know her?"

All at once, David was exhausted. He looked longingly at his bed and the discarded paperback that had landed on the pillow next to his.

Liz followed his gaze and smiled, drawing her own

conclusion. "You're human after all. Come on, then." She took his hand.

David snatched it back. "What?" he asked again. He felt dizzy, faint. The chill inside him was spreading. It must have shown because even Liz noticed, her brow wrinkling with either concern or irritation—David wouldn't have wagered on which.

"Are you all right?"

"Who says I'm not human?" David asked. Or he tried to, anyway. He wasn't sure the words came out correctly, if at all.

"Do you do this every time someone kisses you?" asked Liz.

David swayed on his feet. The air in the room seemed cold to him suddenly; it moved around him like a stiff breeze, trying to push him over. He wouldn't be able to stay standing much longer.

Liz took his hand again, and this time he let her keep it; the warmth of her touch felt nice. "So cold..." David mumbled, and something ran across his memory like a rodent, all sharp claws and too quick to catch.

"You need to sit." Liz pulled David toward the bed and he stumbled after her, nearly tripping over his own feet, but he managed to keep from all-out falling onto the mattress; instead, he climbed up like a child and laid his spinning head on the pillow, closed his eyes against a wave of nausea.

Then popped them open again.

The Michael Crichton book was on the other pillow, swimming in and out of focus. But one thing David saw with complete clarity: a hair.

A long auburn hair on the pillow where Andra had lain that morning.

David reached over and plucked it from the linen. "'Cate..."

. . .

IN THE DARK, Andra's eyes flew open, and for a minute she couldn't remember where she was. She'd been dreaming. Someone beside her in the bed, sobbing into her chest like a bereaved child, and Andra had put an arm around him, gathered him close... She fancied she could still feel the silkiness of his hair as she stroked it in an attempt to soothe him. But of course there was no one there now. It had only been a dream.

Groping for a lamp, only to recall belatedly that there was no light on that side of the bed, Andra rolled and stretched the other way until her fingers found the switch and the antique replica flared on. There was also no digital clock in the room, so Andra found herself squinting at the overwrought gilded thing on the fireplace mantel as she tried to figure out what time it was and why she was awake.

Not even two a.m. She hadn't been asleep very long.

Andra listened for the sound of what must have woken her, but there was nothing but the hiss of silence. No one in the hallway, no party in a room around the corner. Nothing.

Except...

Andra sat up, threw back the sheet. Was there a robe in the room? Where would it be? She zeroed in on the wardrobe, pulled the robe from its hanger, and was out of the room before she'd finished tying the belt, though she soon found herself wishing she'd stopped to hunt for some slippers; despite the carpet, the long-suffering AC kept the house cold enough to freeze Andra's toes.

Andra couldn't completely recall the way back to David's room, but luckily she didn't have to rely on memory. The howling guided her around one corner then another, gathering strength and growing louder the closer she came. In any other circumstance, Andra would have thought a storm was brewing, wind whipping around the house and causing the eerie keening sound. But she knew this storm was in her head. She was the only one who could hear this cry.

Another corner, and Andra's attention was immediately drawn to a door on the left. The wailing dropped then, as a wind dying down, remaining steady but not as loud. Andra stopped and knocked.

"David?"

The door opened. "You're not Henry," Liz said.

A strange numbness began to spread through Andra, a kind of seasickness akin to her feelings on the set the previous afternoon, and for a second she considered just turning around and going back to her room. But the whine in the back of her skull reminded her of her duty. "No," she agreed, "I'm not Henry. Is David...?"

But Liz was typing furiously on her mobile phone. "What's taking him so long?"

Andra stood there as Liz continued to block the doorway. Andra was trying to decide whether to push past and attend to David—or whatever in him was producing that agonizing cry (now more of a thin screech; the closer she got, the quieter it became)—or leave and wait for another opportunity to do her work, when a somewhat breathless Henry rounded the corner.

"Thank God," Liz huffed and finally stepped back. Andra waited for Henry to enter before following.

"He's sick or something," said Liz, gesturing helplessly at the figure on the bed. David was laying on his side, curled in on himself, his back to the room so they were unable to see his face, and Andra's dream came flooding back, her body washed again with the sensation of it.

"Mr. Styles?" Henry asked, taking an uncertain step forward.

"He got dizzy," Liz went on. "Sort of like he was going to faint." She darted a look at Andra out of the corner of her eyes and added, "I mean, I *do* have that effect on men, but we'd barely started."

Andra turned to her with as serious an expression as she could muster. "He probably isn't used to it in concentrated quantities," she said dryly.

Henry, meanwhile, continued to creep toward the bed. "Mr. Styles? Are you all right?"

"Maybe it's something he ate," Liz offered.

"Is it your stomach, Mr. Styles?" Henry dutifully asked. "Do you need some water?"

But David remained still and decidedly uncooperative. The wailing in Andra's head had been reduced to a quiet but steady whimper.

Henry stopped short of touching David, or even leaning in for a look. Instead, the young assistant turned to the women and said, "I think we need Walter."

"Oh, God, Henry. Really?" Liz asked. "Just call the on-set medic."

"Why didn't you?" Andra asked her, and Liz frowned at her impertinence.

"I don't know his number."

For a minute they all stood there. Andra didn't really want an audience for her work, but she couldn't think of any way to oust the others, either. She was considering her options when she realized, once again, that the howling had ceased. She looked hard at David. "I think he's asleep."

Henry gathered his courage and craned over David's figure for a better view. "I think you're right."

"No, no, no," Liz said. "No. He was sick. I had to put him to bed. Like a baby."

The dream flashed through Andra's mind but she shrugged it away.

"Well, he's asleep now," said Henry. "Maybe he'll feel better in the morning." And feeling ever braver, Henry reached over David and took the book off the neighboring pillow, never noticing as he drew it away he was pulling a stray strand of hair with it. A hair that had been held, in part, by David's outstretched hand.

David's eyes opened as the thread of hair slipped out of his fingers. "No," he mumbled, his fingers flexing, working to recapture what they'd lost.

Henry stopped, the paperback in his hands. "You want your book, Mr. Styles?"

"'Cate," said David, but he was already beginning to blink awake, giving him the look of a man coming free of the fog of a dream. He rolled onto his back, and in the dim light of the one lamp Andra was pretty sure she was the only one who saw the change in David's eyes from stormy slate to brilliant blue as he looked up and scowled at Henry. "What are you doing here?" And then to Liz and Andra, "What are any of you doing here?"

"Well, you know why *I'm* here," Liz told him. "And I called Henry because I was worried about you. But," She tossed Andra an arch look. "Why are *you* here?"

For a split second, Andra was at a loss. Then she reached over and snatched the paperback from Henry's hands. "I just came to get my book," she said, and was gone before anyone could reply.

9

First Andra tried to go back to sleep, but every time she started to drift off, the uneasiness of her previous dream began to crowd in on her once more. Failing sleep, she tried to read. But her mind kept going back to David.

'Cate sounded like Katie but was short for Hecate. But how did he know?

Andra tried to reason that maybe David's rusty Greek was surfacing subconsciously. Then she entertained the idea that maybe she was misunderstanding and he really was asking for someone named Katie.

But neither of those explanations accounted for the eyes.

Andra's hand went to her necklace. She wore it always, aside from taking it off to shower or swim. The top charm—the "C" that so fascinated Alfred—had been given to her by a television personality during a stay in Newport, Rhode Island. But on the longer, lower strand of silver chain hung the mark of Andra's office and peculiar power, an ancient key made of bronze.

It wasn't big, not more than two inches, and Andra kept it

polished because otherwise it left smudges on her, especially when she perspired. And Andra also kept it inside her shirt, if only to avoid questions and curiosity.

But David had known without having seen it, had asked for it, in fact. Or demanded it, rather. Except Andra knew it wasn't really David doing the demanding.

Who or what could know about the key? Was whatever it was a threat to her? To David? Or did it really just need her help? If so, by extension David did also, whether he wanted it or not. Unless to help whatever was inside him would be to harm David?

The questions spun through Andra's head as the room gradually lightened with dawn, a mix of grey and lavender light slipping stealthily over the walls and furniture, and all the little *objets d'art*. And as the sun rose, Andra's eyelids fell, and she finally slept.

DAVID FENDED OFF FIRST HENRY, who seemed determined to thrust water down his throat and kept threatening to call the medic, and then Liz, who finally left in the kind of huff David knew meant he would be made to pay during the next day's shoot. But he was too tired to care. After waiting a courteous minute after Liz's belligerent exit, David locked the door behind her, dropped his robe where he stood, and climbed back into bed. This time he turned off the light.

He wasn't ill, just overworked. And the stress of having this Andra woman turn up hadn't helped things. She would be leaving soon, however, if David had anything to say about it.

And he had plenty to say, at least in his own mind. David fell asleep composing a variety of ways to send Andra on her way and out of his life. Some were gentle. Many were not. Which was why (or so he told himself the next morning) he had such terrible dreams filled with fruitless searches in dark places and what he was relatively sure had been a chase through a cemetery, and awoke not feeling the least bit rested. And late for pre-call brunch besides.

"You look awful," Alfred cheerfully confirmed a little later as David hovered over the buffet options, none of them particularly appealing. "Liz said you took ill last night. I'm surprised you didn't let her nurse you back to health."

"Shouldn't you be in Wardrobe?" David asked mildly. He selected quiche and a side of mixed fruit.

"Shouldn't you?" Alfred countered. He followed David to the table, now unoccupied aside from the crumbs left to testify others had been there before them. "I saved you, by the way. Liz was quite on the warpath this morning, but I told her you *must* not be well if you turned her away. Seemed to mollify her. You can thank me later. Or now." When David remained silent, Alfred added, "I suppose I'm not surprised."

"By what?" Now that he had food in front of him, David didn't want it. But he hated to waste, so he took a forkful of quiche and made himself eat it.

"You're not listening," Alfred chided. "Liz. I'm not surprised you turned her down. She *is* high maintenance, after all."

David swallowed a slice of mandarin orange. Vitamin C would do him good. "You think all women are high maintenance."

"True. But there are few who are worth it. Speaking of which, where is our lovely Andra this morning?"

"Gone. If we're lucky."

"Not very nice thing to say about an old friend you haven't seen in a long while," said Alfred. "Is this because Mac has commandeered her? Feeling a bit jealous are we?"

"He can have her," David said. "Just so long as he keeps her away from me." He punctuated this with a grape and almost choked when it slid dangerously close to his windpipe.

"Well, if you really don't mind…" Alfred began.

David gave up on the brunch and gathered his plate to take to the bin. Alfred remained seated.

"I might have a try with her myself," said Alfred.

David rounded on him. "You'd be a damn fool to cross Mac."

Alfred offered a negligent shrug. "She's free to choose, surely. And I'm more charming than Mac by far."

"What about…?" David wracked his brain. "Tina, was it?"

"A passing fancy. But aren't they all? Although Andra… Something different about that one." Alfred finally stood. "Come on, then. You don't want them more upset with you than they are already."

ANDRA JERKED awake in the way of a person who suddenly realizes deep down that they are very late. What she might be late for, Andra didn't know, but given the amount of light pouring in through the windows that doubled as doors to her balcony, she was definitely late for *something*.

As she kicked free of the sheet, there was a soft thud as something fell to the floor. Looking down, Andra saw her Michael Crichton novel had landed half under the bed. She felt a tiny pang in her breast when she thought about how David had had it on the pillow beside him; he must have been reading it, and she'd taken it away from him. Andra scooped it up. She'd bring it downstairs and give it back to David to finish. A peace offering. She was going to have to get on David's good side if she wanted to solve the mystery of whatever was inside him.

Andra dressed and hastily braided her hair to keep it out of her way and off her neck in the heat. She was just exiting her room, paperback in hand, when Henry came darting around the corner. "Oh!" he said, "I was just coming to—" He glanced over his shoulder. "That is, Mr. MacKenzie... And also Mr. Keenan... Had asked after you."

But not David, Andra noted with a tiny pang. "Are they on the set already?" she asked Henry, and when he nodded, "Can you take me? I'm sure I'd get lost in this place."

The young man relaxed visibly, glad for direction, and began striding forward. Andra had to work to keep up. "And how is David?" she ventured. "Better?"

"He's in Makeup," said Henry, which didn't exactly answer Andra's question, but she decided not to press.

At the bottom of the staircase, Henry hesitated. "Did you want anything to eat? They've cleared brunch, but I could—"

"I'm fine, Henry. Are they in front of the house again?"

"They're filming on the west side today. A garden party scene."

"Sounds like fun," said Andra. She looked at the doors leading to the patio where they'd taken lunch the day before.

"That's the southeastern lawn," Henry told her.

"Oh." But Henry had already darted off to the right, and Andra again had to hurry or risk losing him. "It's a big house," she marveled as they began to pass through rooms, some large enough to host parties of hundreds, others featuring little more than a couple chairs, a piano, and a few potted plants. Andra glimpsed a library—fancy David arguing he had nothing to read with all those books!—and a dining room with a table long enough to host at least two dozen guests. And then they came to a smaller parlor off which was a set of double doors that Henry threw open to reveal a long, covered veranda, finely tiled and marked by large columns, between two of which were a sweeping set of stairs that led down to the expanse of grass that Andra assumed was the west lawn.

Andra would have stopped to soak it all in, but Henry went right down the stairs, and Andra trotted after him; she didn't want to embarrass him by having him turn up empty handed to his superiors. Henry cut across the lawn, which looked set up for some kind of tea-and-croquet event, complete with tables draped in white linen trimmed in lace, little roses gathered into cut crystal vases in the centers. If Andra hadn't known it was a film, she'd have thought she'd stumbled into a wedding reception. Well, a wedding reception in which the celebrants intended to play croquet, anyway.

They passed these decorations, and the hoops and peg driven into the green, and came to the place Mac had chosen for his chair, a vacant one ready and waiting beside him. Some directors might have erected some kind of shade for themselves, but Mac was well known for not wanting anything to block his view or obstruct his light. He'd often been quoted as saying, "If my actors can spend hours in the sun, so can I."

Craig, Andra noted as she and Henry approached, had less fortitude than his superior. His fair skin had already begun to blotch, and his hairline was dark with sweat, his shirt patchy with it as he sat in his own chair, alert and ready to work despite his obvious discomfort. The AD's eyes were on the spot where the actors were congregating prior to rehearsal; a much larger group than yesterday, Andra saw as she followed Craig's gaze, but Alfred and David were not among them.

"We're waiting for the sun to get all the way over the house," Mac said. He waved Henry off and patted the chair beside him as if to entice a cat to a lap. "Of course, it would be nice of Alfred and David to grace us so we could rehearse. You're not too hot? I'll send for an umbrella or a hat or something."

"I'm fine," Andra told him as she folded herself into the

green canvas. "You said it yourself yesterday: I'm used to the heat."

Mac nodded with approval, noticed the book in Andra's hand. "Planning to read? Hate to think we're boing you."

Andra replied without thinking, "It's for David," and when Mac's eyebrows shot up, she said, "He was reading it last night. I mean, it's mine, but I took it with me from his room." She could tell by the way Mac's brow was beginning to furrow and his mouth was beginning to purse that she was only making matters worse.

Andra started fresh. "He was sick. Did you know?"

"No," Mac said shortly. "Will he be able to film today?"

"I don't know. Henry said he was in Makeup with Alfred."

Mac leaned back in his chair and called behind Andra's back, "Craig. Go see how David and Alfred are coming along."

Like a good and loyal companion, Craig jumped from his chair and half jogged toward the house. Andra suspected he craved the AC as much as he wished to be recognized for his hard work. Maybe more.

"If he can't pull himself together... After yesterday morning, and now he might be sick?" Mac groused.

Andra had lost the thread of their conversation. "Who, Craig?"

"David."

Andra felt a little stab of concern. "He's fine. He was just tired last night." Mac was frowning again. "Liz and Henry took care of him."

"Liz?"

"Isn't that her name?" Andra asked.

But Mac was swearing softly under his breath. "I can't have this on my set," he told Andra.

"Have what?"

"If they start something..."

"Who?"

"Liz and David."

The pairing of David and Liz once again brought a tightness to Andra's chest and a queasiness to her stomach. "Well, I don't know if—"

"I mean, if it were someone on the crew, sure, but two stars, it's just impossible," Mac was saying. "When they're happy together, God, it's insufferable, and when they fight—and believe me, they *will* fight—it's worse."

"So what can you do?" Andra asked.

But Mac's attention was on Craig, who was hurrying back to his seat. "Well?"

"Almost done," Craig panted.

"David is okay?"

"Same as ever."

"What does that mean?" Andra asked.

Craig's eyes darted uncertainly to Mac, but the director gave nothing away, so Craig cleared his throat and said, "You know, he's just... His usual self."

"So he's okay," Andra reiterated as she tried to understand Craig's reluctance.

"So long as he's better than yesterday," said Mac, then, "Finally," as he spotted Alfred and David coming down the stairs. "David better be careful not to take on any of Alfred's bad habits."

Andra watched as David followed Alfred over to the congregation of actors. She noted that while Alfred looked cheerful as ever, David was tense, scowling. He towered over his co-stars, hanging back a little, until Liz cut right through the group to get to him.

Mac saw it, too, and gave an audible groan. "Craig! Get them started!"

Only too happy to be of service, Craig called for rehearsal. Andra was surprised at the way her breathing eased when

David stepped away from Liz to find his mark. Then he glanced over at where she and Mac sat and his expression darkened, and Andra's chest tightened again.

"What's his problem now?" Mac asked.

But the scene had started. Andra watched, trying to figure out the gist of the story. Alfred and David exchanged some words, then Liz approached and started to say something, only to burst into giggles halfway through. Mac groaned again.

"That's not part of the scene?" Andra guessed.

"Of course not," growled Mac before shouting, "Liz, honey, we need to get this right before wasting any film on it!" Of course it was all digital, but Mac was the kind of director that didn't credit his actors with knowing the difference.

Liz looked appropriately abashed, though the smile lingered around the corners of her mouth. David, Andra noticed, looked strangely blank, detached from everything around him.

"And let's make sure there's a little bit of activity behind them," Mac went on. "People at a party don't stand in one spot indefinitely. Get some movement going back there!"

Craig nodded, and the next couple walk-throughs went more smoothly. Andra tried not to stare, but she couldn't help observing how serious David appeared, even severe. Was that his character? But then Liz stopped mid-scene and asked, "David, could you...?" She made a gesture, palms up and fingers moving as if to suggest lightness. "It is a flirt, after all."

"She's right, David," Mac shouted. "It's a party, not a funeral. Mr. Hastings is *enjoying* himself. Let us see it."

David gave a short nod to show he understood and performed perfectly in the next rehearsal, at least in Andra's point of view. For as Liz's character batted her lashes and smiled coquettishly, David's Mr. Hastings smiled back, keeping just at the edge of propriety as he answered her dialogue with teasing lines of his own. As the scene concluded with Liz sauntering away, Alfred caught Andra's eye and waggled his brows at her. Andra scowled and turned her gaze elsewhere.

"Fine! Good! Get the cameras ready!" Mac called. He turned to Andra. "You doing all right? Need something cold to drink?" And without waiting for an answer, "Stefan! Diet Coke for Miss Martineau! And bring me an iced chai!"

"We've got this bit to do," Mac went on, "and the croquet scene, and then two table scenes and the wide shots of the party."

"Full day," said Andra, sighing at the idea of being stuck out there, having to watch it all.

"Most of them are, if you want to stay on schedule and within budget."

A skinny blond kid—at least, he seemed like no more than a kid to Andra—rushed over with a couple of clear plastic cups. "Who's Miss Martineau?" he asked uncertainly, his voice breaking with nerves. And before Mac could scold him for incompetence, Andra said, "That's me."

Stefan gratefully handed her the darker drink as Mac all but snatched the chai from the other hand. "Thanks," Andra said, but Stefan was already making his getaway.

The cameras were ready, and the scene was down in a handful of takes. "Beautiful," Mac said as they wrapped, "that's more like it."

But as the actors broke so the croquet scene could be set up, Liz stayed to say something to David and Mac added, "Going to have to nip that in the bud, though. Andra..."

Andra looked over. She'd been lost in her own thoughts of how to deal with David—and whatever else was in there.

"You and David are friends..."

Andra's heart sank to her stomach. But she couldn't start denying it now. And yet she also didn't know how she could possibly answer the interrogation she felt was surely coming.

But Mac didn't wait for more in any case. Nor did he begin demanding Andra and David's personal history. Instead he said, "I need you to stop whatever's going on between him and Liz."

"I don't..." Andra answered automatically then stopped. "I mean, maybe nothing is going on."

Mac gestured to where Liz had put her hand on David's arm, making an effort—an unnecessary one, from what Andra could see—to keep her co-star's attention from wandering as she spoke. "That's not nothing," Mac said. "And the more it turns into something, the more trouble it will be. You don't want dear David in trouble, I'm sure."

Mac was looking hard at her, and Andra realized he was searching for a sign that she and David had some kind of romantic history. Or present, maybe. Andra made it a point to meet Mac's gaze evenly, and he relaxed visibly and took another sip of chai.

"It's really none of my business," said Andra. "David is a grown man; he can make his own decisions."

"You can never trust actors to make their own decisions," Mac informed her. "They're terrible at it. It's why they need so many staff. Look, I just wanted to give you a shot, as a friend, to help him. But I can get Walter to—"

Help. It was what Andra had gone halfway around the world to do, only to discover she was more hindrance. But maybe this was a chance to flip things? Keep David from stepping wrong and ruining his career? And better yet, an excuse to get close enough to figure out what was going on inside him?

"I'll try," Andra said, cutting Mac short as she slipped out of the chair. The canvas had knotted her up, and Andra paused to stretch, standing on tiptoe and reaching above her head, belatedly noticing she was still holding the stupid Michael Crichton novel.

"Charming," a familiar voice purred.

"Alfred," Andra sighed.

"Don't suppose you play croquet?" he asked.

"What?" Andra glanced first at Mac, but he had gone to review something on one of the video assist monitors. She then looked over at the green, cameras and lighting equipment now sullying the view a bit as the crew worked to set things up. Then she let her gaze flick toward the shaded craft services table where David and Liz stood, he sipping something from a Styrofoam cup and she nibbling daintily on a bit of cheese.

Alfred did not fail to discern Andra's interest, even though she was quick—too quick—to turn away and careful to keep her face blank. "Leave the book," was all he said, taking it from her hand and tossing it onto her chair. Alfred then took Andra's arm, much as he had the day before at lunch, and guided her toward the croquet field.

As they came to where the mallets and balls had been left in a heap, Craig came rushing over. "You can't—"

Alfred straightened from where he'd been selecting a mallet and gave Craig a hard stare.

"I mean, you know," Craig looked to Andra, but she was already holding the mallet Alfred had handed to her a minute before.

"We won't hurt it," Alfred said, his eyes never leaving Craig's sweaty, blotchy face. Unspoken in the air hung the suggestion that hurting *Craig* might, however, be quite in the cards.

The menace Andra suddenly felt coming off Alfred sent a shiver through her despite the heat.

Craig clearly sensed it, too, as he backpedaled a bit.

"Right, well, just, you know, put it all back when you're done."

"Of course," Alfred said, all reason and affability now as he flashed his famously white smile.

Craig walked backward a few feet before trusting his back enough to turn around.

"Do you play?" Alfred asked Andra, taking up a mallet.

"No. I mean, I never have. I'm supposed to hit the ball through the..." Andra made a gesture to indicate the hoop.

"Right. And after you've gone through the course, you aim for the..." He mimicked Andra's gesture, but pointed to the peg. "Do you want blue and black or red and yellow?"

"*Two* balls?" Andra asked.

Alfred laughed. "Traditionally, yes. Though some make do with one, or so I've heard."

Andra's head was swimming; she'd always thought croquet was a simple game, something rich people did at parties to keep from breaking a sweat. But it was hot out— Alfred had to be that much hotter in his wardrobe—and the lights and equipment being set up around them didn't help matters. And now Alfred was throwing rules at her for a game she hadn't even asked to play.

"We'll start with one ball each," Alfred suggested. "What color would you like?"

"Blue," Andra answered without thinking.

Alfred smiled as if she'd somehow spilled a secret. "All right. And I'll be red. I haven't a coin to toss, but as you're a lady, I'll say you should go first."

Andra blinked at him. She looked at the pile of croquet balls, bent to grab the blue one. Then stood there holding it with no idea how to start the game. "Do I just...?" She dropped the ball in front of the first hoop.

Alfred sighed. "Put it on the baulk-line."

"The what?" Andra turned in a circle in search of the mythical line.

"It's here." Alfred toed the blue ball away from the hoop.

"There's nothing there," Andra protested.

"Indeed not. No one actually marks the lines; that would be bad form. Now come over here and—not like that," Alfred instructed as Andra positioned herself. "Hold the mallet just so." He demonstrated with his own. Andra attempted to do the same.

"And stand like this," Alfred went on.

"Couldn't we just play golf?" asked Andra.

"I'm not Scottish enough for that," Alfred told her. "No, here, the ball won't go more than two centimeters if you hit like that." He came to stand next to her, and as one of his arms slipped around to adjust her grip and stance, Andra began to marvel at just how often he'd managed to get his hands on her in the short time since she'd arrived. The magazines were right; Alfred Keenan was very smooth, almost hypnotic in a way. Andra realized suddenly that she'd leaned into him as if into an embrace and tensed, drew away.

"Practicing for your next big scene?"

Both Alfred and Andra straightened and turned to find Liz and David standing behind them, and Andra silently cursed the flush she felt spreading over her face.

Although it was Liz who had spoken, Alfred directed his answer to the unsmiling David. "You were neglecting your friend, so I thought I would…"

"Show her a good time?" David asked.

"Teach her croquet," Alfred concluded.

"I don't remember croquet being such a cozy sport," said Liz.

"Shall we play doubles?" Alfred asked.

"You're going to give Craig fits by mussing up his course before shooting," said David.

"Is that a no? I'll even take lovely Andra here as a handicap."

"She's my friend, not yours," David said. He looked as startled by the words as Andra felt. Liz didn't look very happy about them, either, which actually made Andra feel a little better.

"Ah, I see," said Alfred. "If anyone is taking her anywhere, it will be you."

"I didn't—" David began, but Alfred cut him off.

"Liz, you're with me."

"I don't want to play," said Liz. "It's too hot for it." She looked to David for agreement, but he was selecting a mallet from the pile.

"Think of it as rehearsal," Alfred told Liz. "The more you do now, the less yelling Mac will do later." He handed her a mallet, which Liz accepted with a distinct lack of grace.

"It's your ball on the line," Alfred said, and Andra assumed he meant her, though he appeared to be looking at David. Andra stepped forward and tried to position herself the way Alfred had shown her minutes before.

"For God's sake, let me go first," said David.

Alfred clucked in disapproval. "Ladies first, David. You know that."

"Well, don't stand like that," David told Andra.

She straightened and scowled. "Oh? Then how am I supposed to stand?"

"Move that foot, your right one, out a little and…"

"If I step out any farther, I'll lose my balance when I swing."

"If you swing like that, you will," said David. "But if you swing properly…"

Andra tossed down her mallet. "Fine. Play by yourself." Hearing the words coming out of her mouth made her cringe; she knew she sounded childish. But she couldn't seem to help it. So many of her clients had been difficult and demanding, and yet she'd always been able to distance herself from their behavior, never allowing any of it to bother her, never taking any of their harsh words personally. She prided herself on remaining gracious and unflappable in the face of petulance. But something about David Styles rubbed Andra the wrong way, making it impossible for her to ignore his criticisms, though Andra knew what he thought shouldn't matter to her. Now *she* was the one being petulant.

To his credit, David looked chastened, if also slightly indignant; Andra supposed he found public displays of temper distasteful. "I was only trying to help," he told her, his tone somewhat strangled as he attempted to maintain a placid exterior. The veneer he was famous for in interviews was beginning to crack.

Andra allowed her gaze to drift over to where Mac and Craig sat, both monitoring the unscripted drama unfolding on the lawn. Then she let her eyes drift to the crew, still setting up equipment, though not so subtly watching them as well. And did she really want the story around the set to be about how she threw a tantrum and stalked off in the middle of a game of croquet? Resigning herself, Andra bent to take up the mallet once more. But she couldn't stop herself from saying, "I don't need your help."

She expected protest, of course. She expected David to point out—not without reason—that Andra most certainly *did* need help playing croquet. But instead he said, "And I don't need yours."

The words stunned Andra. Her gaze met David's, and for some reason she expected his eyes to have gone dark again, maybe because she couldn't imagine that the ever-charming David Styles would say such a thing. But no, David's eyes were as brilliantly blue as ever, bordering on icy.

"Are we going to play or not?" Liz asked. "It's too hot to stand around like this."

David raised his brows at Andra, and with newfound purpose she squared off against the ball and swung the mallet. The ball rolled neatly through the first hoop.

"Nicely done," Alfred offered. "Perhaps you don't need coaching after all."

"You can help me instead, David," said Liz, dropping her ball at the baulk-line.

"Andra gets her bonus stroke first," Alfred reminded her.

Andra looked first to David, whose expression remained stony, then to Alfred, who was as amused as ever by the proceedings. Then she risked a quick peek over at Mac, whose grim expression reminded Andra that she was supposed to be helping David by breaking him free of Liz. In fact, Andra told herself, she was supposed to be helping David in any number of ways—that was the call of a K-Pro, after all—and appeared to be failing on all fronts.

As Andra chewed her lip in uncertainty and poised herself for another swing at her ball, a hand touched her bare arm, causing her to jump. David drew back quickly, as though she'd burned him, but the touch of his fingertips lingered on her skin, oddly cold and tingly, and Andra mindlessly rubbed at the spot to warm it again.

"Sorry," said David quietly as he watched her hand brush his touch away. "But you're aiming for the wrong hoop."

"But that's the closest one," said Andra.

"You have to go in order. You..." David's voice trailed and he began blinking rapidly in the way of someone whose eyes are adjusting to sudden light or dimness.

"David?" Andra asked.

"I told you it was too hot for this," said Liz. "Now look, he's going to relapse."

Andra put a steadying hand on David's arm and peered up

into his face. David's eyes were like a summer sky with rain-clouds moving across them, a strange activity of light and dark.

"Let's get him settled someplace cool and shady, shall we?" Alfred suggested, taking up station on David's other side and beginning to lead his co-star toward the house. Andra started to go, too, but stopped when Mac called for her. She turned and saw him waving her over, and as Andra stood torn between honest concern for David and her need to discover what was inside him, and the need to respond to Mac, Liz passed her, muttering, "Whatever he's come down with, I hope it's not catching."

10

As in his dreams from the night before, David knew he wanted something. And he was vaguely aware that the thing he wanted was getting farther away. Even as Alfred pushed him toward one of the chaise lounges on the veranda, David was twisting to see over his shoulder, trying to discern what the missing piece might be and where it lay.

Because that was exactly what it felt like: something missing from inside him.

But as he turned around, all David saw was Liz's scowl, though she turned on the star wattage when she realized he was looking. "Feeling any better?" she asked.

"Not really. But then, I didn't feel bad to begin with." David resisted Alfred's urging and remained on his feet.

"Didn't you?" asked Liz. "You certainly looked it."

"Charming as ever, Liz, my darling," said Alfred, finally succeeding in knocking David off balance enough that he was forced to sit down lest he fall over entirely. "There you are." Alfred peered into David's eyes as if playing doctor, looking for signs of illness.

David shoved him away. "Stop that."

"You've been funny ever since your friend arrived," Alfred said. "Not that we mind; it makes you more interesting. But also difficult to work with."

"She should go," Liz added ungraciously as she took a seat on the neighboring chaise. "She's distracting everyone. I mean, look at Mac, for God's sake."

The three of them took a moment to gaze over at where Mac was gesturing emphatically with his hands as he lectured Andra on some point or other.

"I like her," Alfred said after a moment.

"You like everyone," Liz remarked, and Alfred shrugged.

"There's something different about her." He turned to David. "How did you meet?"

David massaged his face, trying to get blood moving under his skin; he felt as if he were turning to stone. He needed...

"Leave him be, Alfred," said Liz. "They've had some kind of row."

"Have you?" Alfred asked David.

David stopped rubbing at his brow and looked again to where Andra sat beside Mac. Something silver at her neck flashed in the sunlight. How had he missed it before? She'd been standing right in front of him. "That's it," he said, rising from the chair.

Alfred's gaze followed David's, his dark eyes lighting with interest. "Is it?"

"Alfred, don't encourage him," Liz said, then as David started for the stairs, "Where are you going?"

David ignored her and tried to ignore Alfred when he caught up as David crossed the lawn. But then Alfred said, "She's not just going to give it to you."

David stopped short. "You know what it is."

Alfred halted as well. "I know a lot of things. Chief among

them is the fact that Andra will not willingly part with that necklace."

"I need it," David told him. He wouldn't have been able to explain in that moment *why* he needed it, but he knew he did. And if David expected Alfred to ask why, he was disappointed because all Alfred said was, "I know."

And then Craig called for rehearsal.

"Later," Alfred said when it became apparent David might balk at returning to work before satisfying himself with either the necklace or, at the very least, a solid explanation. Taking a fistful of David's sleeve, Alfred led him back toward the croquet lawn. "Later," he said again. "Right now you need to focus. Don't give Mac any more reasons to dislike you."

David pulled his arm free of Alfred's grasp. "He dislikes me?"

"He certainly isn't in love with you at the moment."

"Because of yesterday?"

"In part," said Alfred. "And because of Andra."

"I don't—" David began but they'd reached the croquet lawn, and Craig was bustling around them, waving Tina over to touch up their makeup. David grew still as Tina stood on tiptoe to daub at his face. When she paused to check her work, she asked, "What's wrong with your eyes?"

Craig overheard and rushed over. "What?" he asked. He scrutinized David for what seemed to the actor like longer than absolutely necessary, then declared, "There's nothing wrong with them."

"Sure there is," Tina insisted. "That's not the right color. Do you wear contacts?" she asked David.

"No..." David glanced around for Alfred, wondering whether his co-star had any answers to this particular puzzle, but Alfred was having his hair tidied by Diane.

"The right color?" Craig echoed. He prided himself on

knowing everything about his job, down to the most flattering angles for each actor, but found himself at a loss when confronted with this bit of trivia. "They're blue. That's right, isn't it?"

"But they're usually much brighter," said Tina.

David shifted from foot to foot like a restive horse, not enjoying the examination.

"That's just the lighting," said Craig, feeling much more in his element. "David, come stand in the sun a minute."

David obediently followed the AD to a patch of sunlight, Tina trailing behind them, and waited for approval of his eye color.

"It really isn't right," Tina said, then asked David, "Do you feel all right?"

David heaved an exasperated sigh. "I'm fine, aside from this heat."

"Well, he can't have different eye colors in different scenes," Craig half whined. He stole a fearful glance in Mac's direction; how to explain this problem?

Tina pulled a small mirror from the pocket of her industrial-style apron and held it up to David's face. "You tell us: aren't your eyes normally lighter than that?"

David inspected himself the glass, blinking as it flashed in the sunlight. He knew his own face well enough, was the kind of sentimentalist to keep a bevy of old photographs tucked away in albums (separate from the scrapbook clippings of professional photos and interviews), and in all of them his eyes were the brilliant blue of clear sky. But in the mirror those eyes—the familiar shape, the neatly trimmed brows and long lashes—were now the stormy slate color of an unhappy ocean. And what was worse than his famous blue eyes *not* being their celebrated shade of blue was the fact that David had the uneasy feeling that something or someone other than him was looking through them.

David let out a tiny moan, and Tina turned to Craig in some triumph and said, "I told you."

"Alfred!" David shouted.

Alfred disengaged himself from Diane's ministrations and sauntered over to join Craig and Tina, who continued to peer and squint at David the way some people do at paintings in museums, as if closing their eyes a bit would actually make him clearer. "What are we looking at?"

"His eyes," said Tina.

"What's wrong with my eyes, Alfred?" David asked. "Why aren't they the right color?"

"Well..." Alfred's gaze darted to Craig and Tina. "An old acting trick," he told them, "if you don't mind." It was a dismissal, and though Tina left with a pout, Craig shuffled away relieved someone else could shoulder the burden.

"Alfred," David said again once the others were gone. "How do we fix it?"

"Is that all you're worried about?"

"Keeping my job is what I'm worried about," David snapped. "My eyes are my best feature; all the fan sites say so."

Alfred looked over at where Mac and Andra sat. "You'll need to get rid of her then. He's awake now, and as long as that key is anywhere near you, he's going to be looking for it."

"He who? What key?"

"We don't really have time for that, do we?" Alfred asked, starting for Andra. "I'll take care of it."

"I've thought of a better way to handle it," Mac told Andra.

She was barely listening, her mind wandering as she watched David, Alfred and Liz take shelter on the veranda.

"Handle what?" Andra asked absently as she tried to discern what the shadowy figures were doing up there. Was David all right? Was the thing inside him hurting him? She needed to move more quickly, finish this job.

"This thing between David and Liz. Aren't you even listening?" Mac asked. "I had Henry make a phone call."

Andra finally turned to regard Mac. "How is a phone call going to help?"

But Mac's lips stretched into a thin, secretive smile. "You'll see."

Over on the croquet lawn, Craig was shooing the stand-ins away from the light meters. Sudden and purposeful movement drew Andra's attention; David, followed by Alfred, was making a direct line for where she and Mac sat. Andra didn't like to admit the skipping pace her heart adopted at the sight of him coming toward her.

But then David stopped to say something to Alfred. And Craig called for rehearsal. And Alfred dragged David over to the set.

"You should consider staying," Mac said.

"What?" Andra asked. "What do you mean?"

"I could give you a permanent job. No more running here and there at the beck and call of random strangers, at least half of whom you don't even like."

"I like more than half," Andra protested. "And anyway, if it were that easy, I'd have settled somewhere a long time ago. But it's not like I can turn it off. They call and I go."

"But what if I'm calling?" Mac asked.

"You're fine," Andra insisted. "You made good for yourself, just like you wanted."

"And what does David want?" asked Mac.

The question jolted Andra, and she found herself studying Mac's face as she tried to discern how much he really knew about why she was there. At the same time, she was unwilling to admit she had no idea what David wanted or how to help him, that what he most likely wanted was for her to leave, and that her leaving might actually be the only way to help him… Except that Mac had threatened to release David if she did leave. *What a disaster*, Andra thought.

"Now what?" Mac sighed, and at first Andra thought he was talking to her, but looking up she realized Alfred was on his way over. And instead of his usual strolling pace, he was moving like a cannonball, an uncharacteristic frown fitted onto his face as he stopped in front of Andra's chair.

"You need to go," he said simply.

Andra blinked up at him, and Mac barked, "Alfred!"

Alfred turned to Mac, unperturbed by the director's ire. "If she doesn't, you won't get this scene. David can't do it with her sitting here."

"Then he won't do it at all," said Mac. "Get him over here. Craig! Where's Craig? We need to find a new—"

"No!" Andra yelped. She stood up. "No, really, it's fine. I'll go in and cool off for a bit." She waggled the paperback and forced a smile. "I've got a book and everything."

Alfred placed what Andra supposed was meant to be a reassuring hand on her back, but it took all of her willpower not to swat his touch away. Craig, meanwhile, had begun trotting in their direction, only to have Alfred wave him off again. Craig paused, doglike as ever, looking between the star and the director, then slunk back to the set, though he made a point to get a Mac-like jab in. "We don't have all afternoon, Alfred."

"That's Mr. Keenan to you," Alfred told him, and Andra couldn't be sure he wasn't joking. From the look Craig shot Alfred, she surmised the AD didn't know, either.

"You seem to have taken to being my tour guide," Andra said as they walked back toward the house.

But instead of the light and jovial reply she had come to

expect from him, Alfred only said, "You really should leave, you know."

Andra knew it was true, of course, but hearing someone else say it hurt her in an unimaginable way. Her breath caught in her chest for a moment, and she had to concentrate on her steps in order to continue walking. "I would have," she finally admitted. "I would have gone yesterday, but..."

"Mac," Alfred put in grimly. He surprised Andra by detouring away from the stairs and the veranda, turning to take her the long way around the outside of the house. "A little more distance, I think," he said.

Andra started to look over her shoulder, but Alfred tutted at her; the farther away they got, the more relaxed her companion became. "You're really worried," Andra marveled.

"Not for unselfish reasons," said Alfred. "For once in a lifetime I have things the way I like them; I'd rather not introduce this kind of mess at the moment."

"Romantic drama?" Andra asked.

But Alfred made a dismissive sound. "I thrive on romance and drama. Once people loosen up, they get interesting."

"And David won't loosen up if I'm around," Andra deduced.

"Oh, he's loosening," said Alfred, "but not in a good way. If he were a painter, he would have cut off an ear by now."

They turned the corner of the house, and Andra found they were at the front, where the previous day's filming had been done. The portico and drive appeared strangely abandoned with no one around; not even a stray production assistant marred the utter stillness.

Abruptly, Alfred stopped walking. Andra got two more steps before realizing it and turning around.

"He wants the key," Alfred said.

A strange flutter of panic moved in Andra's chest. And yet at the same time there was an easing, as if a hefty stone had been removed from her sternum; she was grateful to discover she was not alone in the knowledge that David's problem was something more than heat stroke.

"And you know I don't mean David," Alfred added.

The momentary relief froze solid inside her.

"Now, I need David Styles front and center and completely present to finish this damned movie," said Alfred. "And you and that key as far from the set as possible. No matter what Mac says or does to keep you next to him."

"Who are you?" Andra asked, her mouth suddenly dry.

"Oh, 'Cate, has it really been so long?" Alfred smiled like an indulgent uncle, but his dark eyes remained hot and fierce and just the wrong side of friendly. "It's me, sweetheart. Dear old Dionysus."

INTERSTICE

She comes to a crossroads, four paths branching outward from the one on which she's been running like rays of starlight. Goddess of crossroads, she chooses one blindly, never stopping, her prize clutched tightly in her fist. What would *he* do with it? Open the gates to war? Or merely wheel the world through a slog of days, months, years? These things would help no one.

Her mind fills with the roar of her supplicants as they beg her to unlock the pathways of opportunity, love, prosperity, hope. She cannot deny them. Else the very sounds of their cries will drive her mad.

She is so lost in these thoughts and the echo of prayers being sent to her that she does not see the figure on the path in front of her and runs directly into it. She would fall backward, but it—he—takes hold of her shoulders and steadies her on her feet.

She parts her curtain of hair and looks at him, hardly taller than she, his own hair wild and curly, as unwilling to be tamed as he is.

"Dionysus," Hecate sighs.

"You're in a rush." The words are light, but Hecate is well aware Dionysus' hands still hold her, and though his eyes glint in a friendly fashion there is something yet dark and grave in his expression. She thinks to step away, but his hands are strong, it will be an effort, and he will notice, those eyes that miss nothing.

"You would look so lovely crowned in grape and fig leaves," Dionysus remarks, and Hecate rolls her eyes; it is the same thing he says to every woman.

His eyes fall on her tightening fists and the gleaming object only just visible in the right one; Hecate perceives the swift frown that bends his lips ever so briefly before he forces his eyebrows up in a mask of comic amusement. "Hermes would have made better work of it."

She scowls. She does not have time for this.

Dionysus becomes serious once more. "Would you like me to slow him down?"

Hecate glances over her shoulder. Her head start has been greatly diminished.

"Leave it to me," Dionysus tells her, and his hands fall from her shoulders. "Go."

11

"What did he do, walk her to France?" Mac grumbled. "Henry! Go find Alfred Keenan and get him out here!" And when nothing happened, no scramble of movement, no responding call of "yes sir," Mac shouted, "And where the fuck is Henry now?"

Stefan was the unfortunate elected to tell Mac that Henry had gone out to the airport. He approached Mac's chair the way a child would a lion's cage at an old-fashioned zoo—the kind where the lion might still get in a swipe through the gaps in the bars.

"He had to go out. Henry, I mean," Stefan half stuttered.

"Out where?"

"The airport?"

"Is that a guess or an answer?" Mac asked.

"...An answer?"

"Oh for Christ's sake, Stefan, just go find Alfred for me, would you?"

And so Stefan rushed off with only a scratch as Mac muttered, "Is Henry even old enough to drive?"

· · ·

"I'M NOT…" Andra began. She took one step backward, then another, before silently commanding herself to stand still.

"Oh, but you are," Alfred assured her. "And I am, and David is, too, despite his lack of integration."

"Integration," Andra breathed, her mind swirling. She tried to clutch at things she knew—the things her great-grandmother had taught her about the family's inherent gifts —but there was a snowstorm in her mind, thoughts blown about like flakes in strong wind. They only melted when she tried to catch and hold them.

Alfred moved forward, and Andra tensed. Should she run? If so, which way? Back to the set, the safety of numbers? But she couldn't risk setting David off again. Or whoever was sharing David's intimately personal space.

And then another question presented itself to Andra: did Alfred know who or what was inside David?

But before Andra could ask or run (whichever came first), their solitude was interrupted by Stefan's arrival. The young man turned the corner and stopped short upon seeing the way Alfred and Andra were squared off against one another as if ready for a fight. "Um, Mr. Keenan? Mac was, uh… He sent me to…"

Alfred offered Andra an apologetic shrug. "You know the way from here, I think."

"Yeah," said Andra, trying to smile for Stefan's sake; the boy's big eyes were gulping in the sight of them, and he was no doubt excited to have such a scoop, which was as good or better than currency on a film set. "Thanks." She added a weak wave, and turned and forced herself to walk, if quickly, around toward the patio and gardens.

She should go. Pack up and leave. Never mind if Mac blamed David and cut him out of the movie; David would be better off with Andra far, far away. And Andra would be better off with Alfred—where did he get off telling her he was Dionysus?—far, far away.

Andra crossed the patio, entered the house, climbed the stairs. Her room was... She began making turns that she thought were familiar, but all the hallways looked alike and none of the rooms had numbers. Dionysus? What good was he when what she really needed was Ariadne and a ball of yarn?

For someone so bad with directions, however, Andra had no trouble with doors. More than once she'd absently wandered away from a hotel reception desk or car rental counter without taking the keys; she had no need of them. (At least, not for the doors. As it turned out, she couldn't magically start a car.) So as she wandered the halls of the estate house, Andra poked her head in this room and that, looking for one that was familiar, until she finally found the room she'd started in almost two days before: David's.

It wasn't hers. Her stuff wasn't there. But it would do for quiet and a place to think.

And anyway, she could leave him the book.

"ABOUT TIME," Mac growled as Alfred returned to the set, but if the actor heard the complaint, he didn't show it. Instead, Alfred merely marched over to his mark and asked, "Are we ready then?"

"We've been ready," Mac told him, motioning at Craig to get things moving.

While the AD bustled about for final checks, Alfred turned to David, who stood next to him holding a croquet mallet. "I think I've succeeded in scaring her off for good."

David blinked blankly at his co-star, and Alfred noted the bright blue of David's eyes had been restored. "And you have no idea what I'm talking about," Alfred sighed. "Marvelous."

He picked up his own mallet and tapped gently at a nearby ball.

"Leave it," Craig snarled as he passed before shouting to Mac, "We're ready!"

"Aren't we just?" Alfred murmured as rehearsal began.

DESPITE THE NUMEROUS DELAYS, they managed to wrap the day at a not-too-ungodly hour. David had been at his best, and the scenes between him and Alfred had gone especially smoothly, a fact that unsettled David a bit, though he wasn't entirely sure why. Two actors could certainly not get along off the set and still work well together; he and Alfred were not the first example of that dichotomy. But something had shifted, if subtly, between him and his co-star, and David couldn't quite figure out what, which made him anxious in the way forgetting something important made one anxious.

Feeling it would be better not to stretch his luck (or patience), David had opted to avoid the usual gathering at dinner and had the caterers build a container he could take up to his room so he could eat in peace. He took one of the plastic silverware packets, a collection of paper napkins, and a can of ginger ale, and absconded with his removable feast before Alfred, Mac—or worse, Liz—could corner him.

Unfortunately, when he got to the door of his room, David's hands were too full to open it. In an attempt to make it work, he juggled one thing and another for several minutes before realizing the door had not been completely closed to begin with.

A peculiar dread started at David's scalp and trickled down his neck and across his shoulders.

He toed open the door.

The lights were off. David brushed at the switch with his

arm; it took four tries before he managed to flip it. The room blazed into being as the meticulously placed lamps came on.

The figure on the bed stirred, and David heaved an impatient sigh. "I thought we'd settled this."

Margie merely waved the Michael Crichton paperback she'd been skimming before falling asleep and said, "Since when do you read this shite?"

ANDRA HAD SAT at the marble-topped vanity in David's room until the shadows had become long on the walls and she'd realized she could no longer see things without squinting a little. She'd spent the time chasing the same few thoughts in circles around her head: she should leave; Mac didn't want her to leave, and if she left he would blame David; she couldn't abandon David without somehow freeing him from the thing inside him; David might be dangerous or mentally ill or both; he and that thing might follow her in search of the key; she could never give up the key; how did Alfred know about the key; *Alfred* might be dangerous or mentally ill or both; she should leave...

And then as the sun had begun to sink behind the trees, Andra had begun to worry David might return to his room. So she'd decamped and gone in search of her things, eventually succeeding in finding the room Mac had made hers. The knowledge that Alfred knew exactly which room was hers made Andra quick to pack. Not that she had much with her to begin with, but after assuring herself she'd gathered all her belongings, Andra fished out her cell phone to find out when the next coach could take her back to London—except the site wouldn't load.

With a groan, Andra stepped out onto the balcony to see if she could get a better signal. She'd seen plenty of people around the set using their phones, and the estate boasted Wi-

Fi, so why wasn't hers working? Was her roaming off? She was checking her settings when a voice called up, "What light through yonder window breaks?"

Grimacing, Andra looked down. And yes, there stood Alfred, clearly deep into his cups and illuminated by the lights that surrounded the house so that he appeared to be on a large, grassy stage.

"It is the east, and Cassandra is the sun!"

"The sun has set, Alfred!" Andra shouted back at him.

"I thought we'd agreed it should leave altogether."

Andra decided against pursuing the conversation; shouting back and forth was ridiculous enough, never mind one of them being drunk besides. She went back into her room and shut the large window that doubled as the balcony door, wrenching the latch closed for good measure. Dionysus indeed. But could he climb up to her room? She had no idea but didn't want to find out.

How seriously could she take his claim? Andra wished her great-grandmother were there to ask. Though Andra knew her power—the abilities handed down, only ever to one child per generation—was derived from Hecate, she would never have claimed to *be* Hecate. A servant of the goddess called to do her work, maybe, but not the goddess herself. *That would be crazy. He's crazy.*

Oh? But if he were crazy, how did he know so much about it? About her, and about whatever was going on with David?

Andra crossed the room, scooped up her duffel. She wasn't waiting around to find out how Alfred Keenan knew about her, or the key, or whether he knew anything else. She would go down to the road and flag down a passing car if that's what it took.

But when she opened the door to make her escape, she found "dear old Dionysus" standing on the threshold. "Jesus!" Andra yelped.

"No, never cared for him much," said Alfred as he pushed into the room, sweeping Andra in with him as a tide would debris. She noted that, for a drunk man, he was remarkably alert. Was that a Dionysus thing?

"I thought you wanted me to leave," said Andra as Alfred stood rooted just inside the door and therefore blocking her exit.

"It's not a matter of want," Alfred answered. "You have to go 'Cate. The longer you're here, the stronger he'll get. If you care about David as much as—"

"Who is he, Alfred? If you're Dionysus, who is David?"

But Alfred only smiled kind of sadly, one corner of his mouth quirked in a rueful fashion. "You don't remember. You never do, even without the wine." Then his expression hardened, and the smile sank to a frown like a boat going under a wave. "You need to go. I can't have all this chaos on my film set."

"*Your* film set." Adjusting the duffel strap over her shoulder, Andra took a meaningful step toward Alfred and the door, and he graciously stepped aside.

But as she passed him, he said darkly, "As long as you're here, he will keep trying."

12

"What's that?" Margie asked, nodding at the take away container David had brought with him.

"My dinner." He set it on the vanity, which was the largest and most convenient surface in the room on which to eat. Taking a seat, he popped open the Styrofoam lid and freed his plastic fork from its wrapper.

"What about me?" asked Margie. David had almost forgotten how whiny she could be.

"What about you?"

"I came all the way out here. By special plane, even."

"And they didn't feed you?" David asked between bites of three-bean salad. "Who invited you anyway?"

"Henry called. Said you needed me."

David abandoned the salad for his chicken sandwich. "He was lying."

"Why?"

"How should I know?"

"I thought you were sick or dying or something," Margie complained. "Since they sent a plane and all."

"Sorry to disappoint you."

"And now you're not even going to offer me dinner," Margie went on.

"It's downstairs. Go help yourself."

Margie bounced up from the bed. "You really are awful, do you know that?"

If David had cherished any rose-tinted memories of their time together, those were beginning to dissipate now, rising into the ether like so much smoke. "I'm hungry. I'm tired. I want to be left alone. If anyone should be offering you dinner, it's Henry, since he's the one who dragged you out here in the first place and for no good reason."

Margie strode to the door. "I'm sure I don't know why I bothered. You can die alone for all I care."

"I'll never be alone," said David bitterly. "Can't seem to get two minutes to myself these days." He opened his can of ginger ale and took a sip, waiting for the sound of the door opening and then slamming shut, but it never came. After a moment, he turned in his chair, just to check Marjorie was still there, that he hadn't missed something.

She was standing with her hand on the knob. Her blond hair (not natural, of course, with the dark roots just beginning to peek through; she was due for a touch up) was longer than it had been last time he saw her, and she'd left it down for a change so her waves (and those *were* natural) trailed over her shoulder and down the back of her floral sundress. She wore too much makeup, as usual, and had put on a little bit of weight but also had more color in her skin, more freckles; she'd been getting sun, fresh air, and it was only this small realization that made David miss her a little. Or rather, he was sorry he'd missed whatever outdoor activities had given her such a glow. It was difficult to be faced with evidence that Margie had gone on living without him.

"You used to be nice," she said.

David had no answer to that. He turned around again and

went back to his salad, and a moment later the door did indeed slam shut.

LIZ HAD SAT through the inane dinner conversation, including Alfred's increasingly bizarre comments, which she could only attribute to his steady intake of wine. Nothing new for Alfred, though he usually kept a level head even when in his cups. The man had an amazing tolerance for the stuff. Wine, anyway. Liz had never seen him drink any other kind of alcohol. No mixed drinks and certainly no beer.

Still, she'd put up with Alfred's disconnected thoughts and the petty gossip of the other co-stars (which she had to admit she liked—the gossip, if not the co-stars), all in the hope that David would eventually appear. Liz had darted glances at the door to the house at such regular intervals that as Alfred was clearing his things from the table he'd said, "He's not coming, darling. Took his dinner up in his room."

Liz cut short her natural tendency to scowl and with thespian skill forced a sweet smile onto her lips. "Who would that be, Alfred, dear?"

Alfred returned her honeyed tones with equally smooth timbre. "Oh, I'm sorry, I assumed you were looking for David."

Liz gave her head a tiny shake, smile holding firmly as if glued. "And where is your newest prize then?"

Alfred offered up the heavy sigh of unrequited love. "David saw her first. It would be ungentlemanly of me to insert myself."

The sneer tore Liz's smile from her face as viciously as one small animal might attack another. "Wasn't stopping you this afternoon. On the croquet green."

"And you saw how neatly I was set aside. As were you," Alfred told her evenly. He didn't wait for Liz to respond, merely turned and walked away to return his plate, silver-ware, and wine glass to the caterers. Liz watched, her ire cut by amazement he could still move in a straight line, only to realize that had been Alfred's most coherent conversation of the entire evening. She tracked Alfred as he went out onto the lawn—a walk? it was already getting dark—and rounded the back of the house, out of sight.

Liz turned her glower toward the door of the house once more, willing it to open, and this time it did, but only to reveal Craig, who stopped stupidly on the threshold and blinked a few times in the way of a person with chronic aller-gies when faced with a broad outdoor expanse. He even stopped to wipe at his eyes. Good Lord. He might have continued to stand in the doorway looking daft if not for two things: 1. The door fell back on him as it tried to close, and 2. Through his bleary blinking, he spotted Liz staring at him and construed it as an invitation to join her.

Liz looked away but not quickly enough.

"Hi," Craig said, taking up the seat Alfred had vacated.

"It's not table service," Liz informed him. "You have to go over yourself."

"Oh, no, I'm not—I mean, I already, you know, I just... The room is just so *small*. I couldn't see spending the whole night in it. I mean, I *will* spend the night in it, obviously, the whole night, I don't plan to move in the middle of the night or anything, but until then, you know, until I'm ready to go to sleep..."

Liz was helpless to prevent her incredulity at this streaming speech from slackening her features, her mouth falling open in amazement as she listened to Craig carry on.

"Did you get a new room? I think Miss Martineau might be moving out of hers, your old one, that is, which should be yours anyway, really..."

"Oh, is she?" Liz asked, a little too loudly. At the other

end of the table, heads swung in her and Craig's direction. "And just whose is she moving into this time?"

A mixture of having been interrupted and hyperawareness of the attention focused on him had the effect of stopping Craig's flow, and for a minute his mouth merely guppied like a caught fish's. "Well, I don't know," he answered at length. "I don't even know if it's true. I just... had heard... a rumor... Worth looking into anyway. Perfectly good room. Even has a balcony."

Liz pushed back her chair with such force the scraping noise it made against the flagstones of the patio was painful. "Takes my room and then my co-star? Oh, I don't think so."

"Which...?" Craig began but Liz was already swishing toward the doors to the house. He turned his question to the remaining cast members. "Which co-star does she mean?"

They all looked askance at him for a moment then went back to their meals and gossip, ignoring Craig outright. Frowning at them, Craig wondered what Mac would say to such obvious lack of respect. He tried a few lines out in his head, but none sounded quite right. Craig rose from the table and went back inside, taking effort with his saunter so as to appear nonchalant. Just in case anyone was paying attention.

No one was.

HE'D SPENT the better part of an hour in the library, ostensibly in search of a book, but really just wishing someone might turn up and want to talk. Never mind the fact that a person going into a library was more likely to want to read and be left in peace. There were no televisions in the house, after all, and most of the rooms were pretty small; the library, then, would have to be The Spot, the place everyone would meet after dinner. It would start very casually, people dribbling in, but before long the room would be crowded with bodies, a-roar with chatter.

Craig didn't know this to be true, exactly. He'd more or less made it up in his head. He'd spent almost every evening in his tiny, cramped quarters, thumbing through the daily papers (stolen from Mac's accumulating and neglected pile) and trying, mostly unsuccessfully, to get the Wi-Fi on his laptop to connect. Alas, his room was too deep in the bowels of the estate's stonemasonry to gather a reliable signal. At the best of times it would go in and out, an exercise in frustration; mostly it didn't work at all.

Thus far during the shoot, Craig had not let this setback sway his determination to be shy—or, as he preferred to think of it, "aloof" in a way that clearly marked the line between his superior position and that of all the other crew. So after dinner each evening, he'd stayed mostly in his Hobbit hole (it made him feel better to think of it that way, rather more cozy). But today on set things had seemed to reach some kind of crisis point, and Craig had begun to suspect his being "aloof" had actually cut him off from a certain influx of information that might be useful. The set might be a living version of the entertainment magazines and daily newsfeeds, if only he could access its human data.

Also, Mac had recycled all his unread newspapers.

So Craig had opted to start his evening in the library. There he'd at least have a choice of things to read while waiting for everyone else to show up.

But after almost an hour of waiting, it began to occur to Craig there was an ever-so-remote chance no one was coming.

Which was when he'd ventured outside. Of course, he hadn't taken a second round of antihistamine because he hadn't planned on going out again that evening, so his eyes and nose began to water almost immediately thanks to the damn garden, the wind off the ocean constantly blowing pollen at the patio. Craig told himself *that* was why he never ate outside with the others, never mind maintaining his professional distance.

He'd seen Liz looking at him as he wiped at his eyes, and felt the sweat spring from his palms and forehead like a fountain bubbling to life. *Be friendly*, Craig reminded himself, and anyway, hadn't they had a nice kind of chat just the night before? And if anyone had inside gossip, it would be Liz. In fact, she was probably at the center of things, would be able to tell Craig what was going on first hand.

He wiped his hands surreptitiously on his chinos and walked over.

Be cool, he told himself again and again. *Be cool, be cool, be cool.*

He was not cool. He was a blabbing mess, and far from getting any good information, he instead spilled the little bit he did know right into Liz's lap. Miss Martineau was leaving. He'd heard it from Stefan, who apparently had heard or seen something between Miss Martineau and Alfred earlier that afternoon. Mac was going to be angry if it were true. And Craig couldn't help but wonder if it would reflect badly on the production as a whole.

This was Craig's continued worry as he left the table and went back to his Hobbit hole. And he still had nothing to read.

LIZ WENT STRAIGHT to David's room. Well, as straight as one could go anywhere in that house, what with its twists and turns. But she knew where David's room was; that much was emblazoned in her brain.

She'd just started to turn the corner into David's hallway when she saw his door open. Liz's heart gave a little leap of anticipation as she mentally readied her ambush. She'd pretend to be lost, of course, looking for... Who? Or what? Liz was still trying to decide when she saw the blond woman step out into the corridor and slam the door behind her.

Now who was *that*?

Liz watched the stranger shuffle off in the opposite direction. Based on the very loud sniffling, the woman was crying. Could David need comforting then? A sympathetic ear and some compassionate arms to fall into?

But it was no good rushing in. No, she'd need to give him a modicum of time to wind down first. Liz glanced down at what she was wearing. Jeans, a singlet—in other words, nothing very exciting. Better to go get freshened up and then launch her campaign.

WHEN ANDRA PASSED the crying woman, she was tempted to keep walking. After taking turn after turn through the labyrinthine corridors, she could finally see the light at the end of the tunnel, quite literally, since the hall she was in opened onto the landing and the stairs that would take her down and out of the increasingly complicated world she intended to leave behind her.

But the stair landing featured a beautifully carved and polished bench topped with a rich red and gold brocade cushion. Perhaps it was expected in earlier days that women would fatigue themselves going up the stairs and would need a rest upon achieving the next level. Or perhaps the owners of the estate were aware their visitors might have spent the better part of an hour wandering and lost and would need a rest upon finding their ways out of the maze. In either case, it wasn't a bad place for a bench, and it was just as good a place for a cry, Andra supposed, at least when no one else was around.

It wasn't unusual for film sets to be full of people crying in corners; experience had taught Andra that well enough, and in most cases the criers didn't want to be disturbed. Andra didn't know *that* so much from experience; it was more of an assumption on her part. But it worked well enough as an excuse to leave the woman alone.

Except, as she passed the sobbing figure, Andra saw something out of the corner of her eye that made her stop. And look.

On the bench, next to the woman, was a Michael Crichton paperback novel.

"My book," Andra said, not meaning to, but it popped out the way thoughts sometimes did when one wasn't actually thinking.

The woman lifted her head, and Andra almost yelped at the sight of a face streaked with makeup. "*Your* book?"

"Well, I... Lent it to a friend."

"David?" the woman asked.

Andra hesitated to answer; the woman appeared to be becoming increasingly upset.

"It was on his bed," the woman went on, her tone laced in accusation.

"Well, I... Left it for him. We're old friends," Andra added, falling back on the lie she and David had perpetuated since her arrival, though whether anyone believed it was another matter entirely.

"Old friends?" the woman asked, her voice rising to an alarming pitch. "Who are you? I've never seen you in my life! And I spent nearly ten years with him, so I should think I know all his *old friends*!"

"You're Margie," Andra realized dumbly. She hadn't recognized David's ex-girlfriend, seen in so many old online photographs during her research, through the mess of makeup and tangle of hair.

"Of course I am," Margie snapped. "But who are you?"

"Andra."

"Well, I never heard David mention any Andra," Margie informed her.

"No, probably not," Andra agreed, taking a step back from the heat of Margie's anger. "I'm just leaving anyway. He can keep the book."

"I don't want your stupid book, and neither does he!"

But Andra was already making for the stairs. "Right, well, whatever."

"Wait!"

Against her better judgment, Andra stopped, though she mentally calculated how likely it was Margie could catch her if it came to that.

Margie drummed her fingertips on the cushion in a show of nerves and thrust out her lower lip so she could blow some wayward strands of hair from her eyes. Under the mask of runny mascara and too much rouge, Andra watched the face work through various iterations of what to say and how to say it to get to the desired outcome. Finally, with a sigh Margie asked plainly, "What's he up to?"

"Up to?" Andra echoed. "How do you mean?"

"He's not acting right."

"Well, he was probably surprised to see you. He doesn't like surprises."

Margie made a noise that was half laugh and half sniffle. "True. Still... He was meaner than he needed to be."

It was Andra's turn to be surprised. "Mean?" she asked. David had a stubborn streak, yes, but from the little Andra had managed to garner, she didn't think 'mean' was a typical trait for him. And clearly Margie didn't either.

"I know he didn't want to see me again, but I only came because Henry made it sound so important. I thought David was really sick or something!"

"Henry?"

Margie rolled her eyes. "Do you always just turn what other people say into questions?"

"Always?" Andra meant it as a joke, but for a moment she thought Margie might burst into a paroxysm. Then suddenly Margie began to laugh.

"I can see why he likes you," Margie said, and Andra found herself wishing it were true. Had she ever had a client dislike her the way David did? No. Andra was sure she wouldn't be capable of doing the work if it were always this difficult, this emotionally painful.

Margie swiped at a cheek and grimaced at the black streak that migrated onto her hand. "Don't suppose there's someplace I could clean myself up? I came so quick, I didn't even pack anything to bring with me."

Andra glanced back down the hallway. "I'm not even sure I could find my room again; this place is a maze. But we could give it a try."

"I don't want to keep you from your bus or…" Margie gave a nod toward Andra's duffel.

"I'm not on a schedule," Andra told her. As they started back down the corridor, Margie asked, "You his new girlfriend then? Or new old girlfriend, if you're leaving?"

"No, just a friend." Andra hazarded a right turn.

"How long have you known him?"

"Sometimes it feels like forever," said Andra, making another turn. "And sometimes I feel like I hardly know him at all."

"Yeah," Margie sighed. "Even after ten years there were days when I was sure he'd turned into someone else entirely. Like Jekyll and Heckle."

"Mm." Andra made a final turn and was relatively certain they'd made it to the hallway her room had been in. It was only then that she remembered she'd left Alfred standing in the middle of said room. The thought gave Andra physical pause, causing her to stop mid-step.

"What's wrong?" Margie asked.

"Oh! I just don't think I have the key anymore."

"If you locked it, you must have the key," Margie reasoned. "And if you don't have the key, it must be unlocked. Which one is it?"

Andra edged down the corridor the way people did in horror movies, Margie close behind her. After a minute, Margie whispered, "Is someone sleeping?"

"Huh?"

"Is that why we're tiptoeing?"

Andra stopped in front of the door she was almost positive had been hers. It was the end of the hallway, after all, the back of the house where the balcony would be. Slowly, she reached for the doorknob, turned it.

"It *was* unlocked," Margie pointed out.

The room was also empty.

"YOU'RE LOOKING FOR HER, aren't you?"

As David stepped out of his room, he found Alfred leaning against the vividly papered wall just outside his door.

"I was just going to throw out my—" David lifted the catering carton and plasticware for Alfred's inspection. "If I bin it in my room, the whole space will smell."

Alfred used his shoulder to leverage himself to full standing. "You should recycle."

"Fine, I'll recycle it. I'm sure they have bins for that, too, somewhere." David started off down the hall, privately hoping Alfred would leave it at that, but not at all surprised to find his diminutive co-star keeping pace at his side.

"And then you were going to go look for her?" Alfred queried.

"Look for who, Alfred?" David asked wearily.

"Andra."

David sighed. "Hasn't she left?"

"Mac won't let her. And he'll blame you if she does leave. I'm sure you can imagine how that might go." They'd come to the landing, and Alfred prepared to follow David down the stairs, but David stopped suddenly, frowning.

"That's her book."

Alfred turned and saw the worn paperback that had been abandoned on the bench. "Was she done with it?"

The sudden ire David turned on him caused Alfred to take a step back. "How the hell should I know?" David snapped, and Alfred could see the colors moving through his co-star's eyes like dark clouds passing over an otherwise clear sky.

"There you are," Alfred murmured, then louder, "You look like you could do with some fresh air, Davey, my boy."

David only stood there, scowling.

"Walkies?" Alfred asked.

The scowl deepened and the eyes darkened.

"You'll have to throw those things out outside in any case," said Alfred. "Might as well go for a stroll."

David stepped over to the bench, picked up the paperback and slipped it into his back pocket. "What do you want?"

"No sense in spending all night cooped up in your room," was all Alfred said. "You don't even have a balcony."

"Thank you for reminding me," David said lightly as he made for the stairs. "We're not friends, you realize."

"I'm aware," Alfred agreed. But it didn't stop him from staying by David's side as they descended, exited, and set off across the lawn into the dark.

LIZ SMOOTHED the front of the eyelet lace dress she'd selected, perfect in her mind for a sultry summer evening, then tapped at the door. Waited. Frowned and cocked her head for any sound of movement within the room. Knocked harder. She was just about to try the knob when movement at the far end of the corridor caught her eye.

A woman was making her way down the hall, her dark head bent forward so that Liz couldn't get a good look at her face. Not Andra, though, and not the blond woman from earlier either, which was just as well, but in any case Liz was not eager to be found looking like a fool in front of David Styles' door. She turned the knob just as the woman stopped behind her.

The door gave, but Liz didn't open it, instead turning to see what this person might want. The woman lifted her head, and suddenly Liz recognized her. From Wardrobe? No, Makeup.

"Tina," Liz said aloud as the name came to her.

"Hi, Liz." Tina's voice was a little shaky, and Liz fleetingly wondered if she were on the verge of tears. But more important, in Liz's mind, was the question of why Tina was coming to David's room, and dressed in such form-fitting clothes? Not that Liz thought Tina had much of a form. Or rather, a bit too much of one; Tina looked all but sewn into her jeans. "Is David in?"

"Why do you want to know?" asked Liz, and Tina took a step backward at the force of her tone.

"I just—I can't find Alfred, and I thought…"

Liz visibly relaxed. "Alfred? But he and David aren't friends, you know. They can hardly stand one another."

Tina's face fell. "They were cozy on the set today, so I thought… And then Alfred promised to meet me in the library…"

"Alfred Keenan is *not* the kind of person to pin a hope on, love; he's not that trustworthy. Anyway, he went for a walk after dinner," said Liz. "He could be anywhere."

Tina mumbled something that Liz assumed was thanks and turned to go. Liz waited a minute before pushing the door to David's room fully open; she hoped her and Tina talking in the hallway outside his door hadn't disturbed him. At least, not enough to disinterest him in a visit from her. Strange things seemed to set David off, but that was part of what made him interesting.

But when she opened the door, Liz saw the room was dark. She flipped the switch for a better look, but the room remained obstinately empty. Liz even ventured for a peek in the bath to see if she might have been lucky enough to catch David in a shower, but there was no one.

With a growl of frustration, Liz exited the room, yanking the door closed behind her. At the end of the hall, she could see Tina's dejected figure just about to turn the corner and made a snap decision. "Tina, wait!"

Tina lifted her bowed head and stopped walking long enough for Liz to catch up. "It's strange," Liz confided in a way meant to bring Tina into her circle. "David is missing too."

"Were you supposed to meet him?" Tina asked. And when Liz only stared, "So maybe they're together after all?"

Liz loosened and gave a tiny shrug. "I think combining our efforts might at least save time and energy. And we'll start with the one person pedantic enough to keep track of everyone on this set."

"I thought *you* were the..." But Tina's voice trailed when Liz stabbed her with a warning glare.

"I may know all the gossip, but I am not my fellow actors' keeper," said Liz. "When it comes to wrangling, we need— "

CRAIG SQUEEZED his eyes shut for several seconds. Then

he opened his left to be sure, closed it again, opened his right to be doubly sure.

But yes, there were two women at his door.

"What are you doing?" Liz asked.

"I just, uh, you know. Allergies."

"We need to find David and Alfred," said Liz.

Craig glanced behind him as if the two actors might be hiding in the tiny space that was his room. "Uh…"

"We usually meet in the library," Tina offered. "Me and Alfred, I mean."

"I knew it!" said Craig, adding, "I must've been there too early."

Tina's brow furrowed and she gave her head a little shake to show she had no idea what Craig was talking about while Liz said, "Your being stupid isn't helpful, Craig. Do you know where they are?"

"No…"

"But they aren't, I don't know, meeting with Mac or something?" Tina asked.

"Not without my knowing about it," said Craig, but even as the words left his mouth, a tiny prick of fear made him wonder. Could Mac be holding meetings without him?

"You know what," Craig went on, "I'll go check with Mac to be sure there isn't anything I—we—don't know about."

"And we'll keep looking," said Liz. "Just be sure to let us know if you find them." She turned to go, Tina hesitating briefly before following suit.

Craig turned this way then that in search of his mobile phone. "Well, I—I don't have your number." But they were already gone.

Andra was simultaneously relieved and concerned. Relieved, of course, not to have to deal with

Alfred, and concerned about what Alfred might be out doing. Bacchanal, perhaps? As she stood in the doorway, trying to decide exactly how concerned she should be, Margie ducked past her into the room, did a quick whirl in search of the bathroom, and made a line for it once she'd spotted the door.

"Christ," Margie moaned, ostensibly at her reflection, her voice an odd and hollow echo as it bounced off the surfaces of the room.

Finally convinced it was safe, Andra stepped inside and shut the door behind her.

"It's a nice room," Margie said as she emerged from the bath, her mascara streaks gone, though now her cheeks were red from having had tissue rubbed vigorously over them. "As nice as David's even."

"Yeah, well, Mac is an old friend," said Andra.

"Mac *and* David? Who *are* you?" Margie plunked herself onto the bed with a little bounce, and Andra realized there would be no swift escape now; Margie was settling in. Andra supposed Margie thought of them as friends now, or at least friendly, with David as a common thread to connect them.

But Andra didn't really have friends. She had clients and acquaintances, but not friends. No one with which to go shopping or gossip over dinners; Andra spent too much time in the whirl of her work to want to be anything more than alone on the rare occasions when she had time to spare.

"Is he sick?" Margie asked when Andra failed to answer the first question. "Henry made it sound like he was on his death bed."

"It's not that bad," Andra said, though the image of a groggy and irritated David curled up in bed flashed behind her eyelids.

"Pushing himself too hard, I'll bet," said Margie. "He takes it all so bloody seriously."

"Probably," Andra agreed before adding, too brightly, "Well! You can have the room if you want, since—"

"Have you eaten?" Margie asked. "Because I haven't yet, and David said there was food downstairs."

"Oh," said Andra, feeling like someone suddenly asked on a date to which she didn't want to agree. But faced with Margie's wide and hopeful stare, rather like an orphaned puppy's, Andra felt she could hardly abandon David's ex-girl-friend to the wilds of a fraying film set. And with Alfred loose to boot. "Have you ever eaten film catering?"

"David likes to keep his personal and professional lives separate," said Margie, which Andra took to be a long form of "no."

"Until now, anyway," Margie went on.

It took Andra a minute to realize Margie was referring to her. "I'm here on business," Andra said repressively.

Margie's eyebrows inched up, as if Andra's protest had only proved her point, and an indignant flare burned through Andra's insides like a torch being lit. But even as her nails bit into her palms, Andra forced herself to douse the fire. After all, Andra reminded herself, Margie didn't know anything about K-Pros or how Andra prided herself on her detached demeanor. Dozens served over the years—strictly in a business sense. Despite the adage, some rules weren't made to be broken.

Andra glanced out the window; it was now full dark. She wondered what time call was in the morning and whether the thick of actors had broken up from their dinners, gone to seek solitude in their rooms, or company in each other's rooms, in that way they had. They might be crowded around a television somewhere watching whatever kind of sport they had in England. Except Andra hadn't seen any televisions in the house. The library? Not likely. Holed up reading the next day's sides?

It didn't much matter aside from Andra wanting to avoid them. But she and Margie needed to eat, as Andra's stomach was beginning to point out quite audibly.

"Is it no good?" Margie asked, causing Andra to jump out of her wandering thoughts. And when Andra only blinked uncomprehendingly, Margie added with an exasperated sigh, "Film set catering."

"Oh. Well, it depends on the caterer."

"Should we go somewhere else?"

The suggestion was appealing on at least one front, but Andra wasn't sure she was ready to sit down to a meal with this woman any more than she wanted to face the cast and crew. Also, she didn't know where else they could go or how they would get there.

"No," Andra finally decided. "We should just..." She was already moving for the door, her hand on the knob as Margie rose from the bed. But when Andra stepped aside and opened the door to allow Margie out of the room, Margie gave a little gasp. Andra whipped her head around for a look, afraid Alfred had returned to spout more warnings or maybe more Shakespeare. Or maybe he'd combine the two in an "Ides" kind of speech. But when she saw the figure in the doorway, Andra relaxed. "Walter."

"Well?" he asked.

"Well what?" Andra countered.

"Is he in here?"

Andra and Margie exchanged glances. Neither needed to ask for whom Walter was searching.

"No," Andra said while Margie merely shook her head.

"Come on then," Walter said, turning to hike back up the hall. "We're going to have to widen the search."

13

"Mr. MacKenzie?"

Mac kept his eyes on the monitor and ignored the hesitant, half-whispered whine in the hopes it would go away.

"Mac?" A little louder now, but no less whiny. With a barely restrained snarl, Mac paused the scene he was reviewing (and if it happened to be that moment on set two days before when Andra had taken David's hand and then he'd clasped hers, that was no one's concern but his own) and turned to see who dared to bother him.

"Craig. You're still here?"

For a split second Craig was nonplussed. He concluded the question was rhetorical and decided to move on. "We can't find Alfred or David."

Mac had already returned his attention to his monitor. "Who let you in?"

"Your door was unlocked."

Mac sighed, his eyes glued to the screen in front of him. He still sat where he'd eaten his dinner—on his balcony, alone, which had not put him in a good mood. Nor had seeing Alfred's clumsy attempt at romancing Andra two balconies down pleased him; indeed, Mac had been unable to finish his steak after that. Now Craig was here saying…

Mac snapped to attention, jamming the pause button on his monitor so violently that Craig gave a little hop backward.

"What do you mean Alfred is missing?" Mac demanded.

"Well, I mean we can't find him. Or David."

"And where's Andra? Miss Martineau," Mac clarified in case the AD didn't recognize Andra's first name. Mac wasn't sure what Craig did or didn't know; it had never mattered until now.

"I don't know." Craig stopped to absorb this new information. "I thought her name was Katie."

But Mac was on his feet now, going for the door. "When and where were they last seen?" He didn't bother waiting for an answer; instead he swung himself out the door and into the claustrophobic corridor, Craig hot on his heels like the good and loyal dog he was.

"I don't know," Craig said again. "I mean—"

"Then how do you even know they're missing?" Mac snapped. He stopped at a door, knocked. "Andra?"

Craig hovered at Mac's shoulder. "Well, Liz couldn't find David, and then Tina couldn't find Alfred, and—" He was prepared to launch into the whole story but Mac cut him short.

"If David has any sense, and I'll admit that's a matter of some debate, he's probably hiding from Liz and nesting with that Meggie tart of his. Andra?" Mac tried the door; it wasn't locked. He pushed it open, reached blindly for the light switch, and surveyed the room.

"No signs of a struggle," Craig offered, and Mac tossed a glare over his shoulder. Craig didn't notice; his eyes were on the room. "You think she's with them?"

"The last time *I* saw Alfred, he was lobbing Shakespeare at Andra from the lawn below her balcony."

"Really? When was that?" asked Craig.

"An hour and twelve minutes ago."

Craig decided not to ask how Mac knew so precisely and without even looking at his watch besides. "But what about David?"

Mac took ginger steps into the room, almost tiptoeing, as if entering a shrine. "What about him?"

Craig remained in the doorway. "He's missing too," he reminded the director. "Did they all go together, do you think?"

Mac inched his way around the bed, craned his neck to get a glimpse of the bathroom. Then suddenly he strode into the bathroom; Craig heard the snick as Mac flipped the light on. A few seconds later Mac reappeared with a wad of smeared tissue in his hand. "She was crying. A lot."

Craig knit his brow at the colorful crumps. "Does she wear that much makeup?"

"You're missing the point, Craig. Where would he have taken her?"

Craig bit back the urge to point out that his attention to detail was what made him a good assistant director and asked, "What makes you think he—or they—took her anywhere?"

Mac only stared at Craig as if the AD had begun speaking another language. "We need to find Andra."

"Does she work for the studio?" Craig blurted. "Is that why we'll be in so much trouble if anything happens to her? I mean, not that I think Alfred or David would—"

"What are you talking about?" Mac asked. "Andra is one of my oldest and dearest friends."

"So... She doesn't work for the studio?"

Mac stared hard at Craig for a long moment before asking, "Shouldn't you be back at the hotel?"

TINA HAD FOLLOWED Liz through the house, mostly because Liz seemed to know what she was doing, and also in large part because Tina was afraid she might otherwise get lost in the endless hallways that appeared to loop back on one another like some kind of funhouse. "Stanley Kubrick should have filmed here," Tina muttered as they took yet another turn.

"What?" asked Liz in a tone that suggested she didn't actually want or expect an answer. Tina kept her mouth shut, and a minute later Liz's mobile phone rang. Tina waited while Liz answered it, trying not to listen, though it was difficult not to overhear when Liz began yelling, "Why are you asking *me*, Walter, when it's *your* job to keep an eye on him?" And then, as Liz held the phone away from her ear and frowned at it, "He hung up."

They started walking once more and eventually came to a lounge that was beginning to fill up with crew members. Liz marched up to a large, bearded man perched on the arm of a sofa and asked without preamble, "Where's David?"

The man turned slowly from where he'd been chatting with a fellow technician, and the dull roar of the room quieted to a murmur as everyone else pretended not to be watching or listening but wanted to make sure they could all still hear.

"Do you even know who I am?" the man asked, his voice low and gravelly.

"You're a…" Liz's right hand moved in the air as if to conjure the appropriate response.

"Look around you, little miss," the man went on. "You see any of your actor friends in here?"

Tina stepped forward. "Mike," she said, "you haven't seen Alfred around, have you?"

Mike shot another sharp look at Liz, but under Tina's beseeching gaze relented. "Not since we wrapped, sweetheart. He stand you up?"

"Liz says he went for a walk after dinner. Now that's it's dark, though, I thought he might've come in."

"You shouldn't be wasting any time or worry on him anyway," Mike told her. "Alfred Keenan only ever looks after one person."

"He's not like that, Mike," said Tina.

Liz snorted. "And what about David?"

Mike's eyes slid in Liz's direction and his expression cooled. "Haven't seen him."

Liz's eyes swept the room, and nothing but unfriendly faces looked back at her. Turning on her heel, she said, "Come on then, Tina, time to take this to the great outdoors."

CRAIG TRAILED Mac through the labyrinth that was the house. A man of action, Mac was not given to resorting to phone calls or text messages; after all, he was a firm believer in doing things yourself if you wanted them done properly.

Craig, meanwhile, would have texted or called someone—anyone—if he'd had the numbers. But somehow he always managed to be out of the loop on those things. He would almost have sworn the contact list was being kept from him, though Craig was practical enough to know better. He had a copy of it. Somewhere. He just hadn't been able to locate it. Ever.

A group of crew members had gathered in one of the lounges to listen to a radio broadcast of a cricket match. Craig naturally balked at the doorway, ready to slink away with no one there the wiser, but Mac strode in and managed to ignore the furrowed brows and frowns his interruption won him.

"Has anyone seen our stars?" Mac asked.

After several seconds of exchanged glances, shrugs, and shaking heads, a grip said, "Well, we saw Liz Hellmann. All dressed up like she might be going out somewhere."

Craig's cheeks reddened. He leaned in toward Mac and whispered somewhat desperately, "But we aren't looking for—"

"Where and when?" Mac asked the grip. Stuart, Craig recalled, and this was only his second movie; the kid's grandfather had been an FX artist of some renown.

Stuart made a face that fell somewhere between sly and embarrassed. "Here. A little while ago. She was looking for David." He darted looks at his crewmates as if to discern whether he'd overstepped his bounds by volunteering so much information.

"Well, and he's probably hiding from her," said Craig, echoing Mac's earlier comment in an attempt to sound knowledgeable about the situation. But now Mac whipped around to frown at him, even as a knowing wave of smirks and grins swept the room.

"Let's hope she hasn't found him," the director said. "Christ, what a disaster. And after we paid to bring that girl of his out here besides." He turned from the lounge without offering so much as a thank you to Stuart for his insight, and Craig tried to wave something that conveyed appreciation and apologies simultaneously and was summarily ignored.

"Should have brought someone for Liz, not David," Craig said under his breath, and Mac stopped short.

"What?"

"No," Craig said quickly, rather like the victim in a horror movie right before the killer struck. "No, nothing, I didn't say anything."

"But you did," said Mac. "And you're right. Damn it. That's exactly what we should have done." And as Craig blinked his surprise, Mac turned to walk again. "You may have the makings of a director yet, Vauderhagan.

"We've covered the house," Mac went on. "Let's go outside."

AS THEY EXITED the glowing halo that surrounded the house courtesy of the spotlights hidden in the shrubbery, the lawn and air around the house seemed to grow darker. And while the grass had appeared level and benign that afternoon, David now found it to be slick and more sloped than he remembered. Treacherous.

David's nightmares returned in vivid form as he and Alfred made their way through the dense black that had settled over the grounds like a shroud. The feeling of looking for something—something or someone important—returned to David with the force of a blow, even as a chill began to run over him. Something about the darkness wasn't right. Looking up, David couldn't even see the stars; there was nothing but unbroken blackness. Unconsciously, David drew closer to Alfred, if only to avoid losing him and becoming stranded.

Beside him, Alfred looked up uneasily. "This dark..." he murmured.

Then, like landing lights along a runway, the tiny lights for the garden began to wink into view where they lined the beds and thus marked the wide, grassy paths. David glanced over his shoulder at the hulk of the estate and wondered at the ocean of black between it and its gardens. A trick of his mind, he decided. It was not as far as it looked. It couldn't be.

Alfred caught David looking and his lips stretched in a way that was more grimace than smile. David waited for whatever clever remark would accompany the expression, but Alfred remained silent, his dark eyes scouring the black fog that enclosed them. That, more than anything, tightened the knot of not-quite-right that had begun to tie itself in David's stomach. He tried to trace the events that had led them to that moment, what exactly had precipitated their walk, and found he couldn't. The fog was in his mind as well as around his person.

As they reached the path, David stopped walking. "What are we doing, Alfred?"

Alfred stopped two steps beyond him and turned, his grimace becoming a full-fledged glower. "Don't fuck with me, Janus."

David looked over his shoulder again, but he and Alfred were the only two people present, at least from the little that David could see. "What?"

"You *would* do this now," Alfred growled. "You two-faced son of a bitch."

David's mind scrambled backward. Had he and Alfred had a fight he couldn't remember? "What?" he asked again, mostly to buy time to think.

Alfred's shoulders sagged in resignation. "Oh, for..." He took the two swift steps to close the space between them, causing David to flinch, then reached around David to pull the tattered paperback from his pocket. "Her, remember?" he said, holding the book in front of David's eyes. "You've called her all this way. Are you going to let her leave without getting what you want first?"

The book blurred in David's vision. His chest tightened and his head felt suddenly fuzzy inside, like on days when he went without eating. Had he eaten dinner? Yes, he recalled, following the thread backward, he'd just thrown out the carton. His chronology was sideswiped by a flash of croquet, of being angry about something, or had that simply been the heat? It was hours ago in any case. Surely he'd eaten since then. Yes, of course, he'd just finished his dinner when Alfred turned up at his room. The carton. The bin.

David put his hands to his head in an attempt to hold his thoughts together.

"Come on, then," Alfred half taunted, waggling the paperback as he began to walk away deeper into the garden. "Let's get this over with."

"I DON'T UNDERSTAND," Margie kept saying as they wended their way first through the house then around its perimeter. Walter went from phone call to phone call, speaking first to Henry, then to the estate manager, then to the head of the Teamsters to make sure David hadn't taken a car, then back to Henry, and so on in cycles. He called Liz once to see if maybe David had visited her room—a mistake he did not make again.

"David's not much of a wanderer," Margie went on. "More of a homebody, really, unless there's some…"

While Margie's constant stream of awed confusion went on in Andra's left ear, her right was treated to Walter's, "Yes, Henry, that's exactly what I'm saying. If he *is* suffering from some kind of exhaustion, we need to get him treatment."

"I mean he's totally attached to his mother. He's her baby, and good God, let me tell you…"

"It would be better if we could isolate him, do this quietly before it becomes a headline."

"Shut up! Both of you!" Andra stopped in her tracks, and Margie and Walter stopped too, Walter holding the phone slightly away from his ear so that Andra could hear Henry asking, "Uncle Walter? Are you still there?"

"I need quiet so I can concentrate," Andra told them.

"Concentrate on what?" asked Margie, but Walter merely moved away until he came up hard against the side of the house. Andra supposed years of working with the strange personalities common in show business had left him jaded; nothing surprised him anymore, no use in asking, but he also knew when to stand clear.

Andra closed her eyes. She heard Margie inhale and held up a hand to stop the coming question. Margie let out the breath and was silent.

It was an old skill, one Andra almost never needed to think about any more, but under the current circumstances, which were unusual in the extreme, she needed the quiet. Andra stretched her senses like invisible fingers, reaching in every direction. She was listening for the sound of him, the beacon that had called her there in the first place. If David was looking for her—and Alfred seemed to believe he was or would be—then he, or whatever was inside him, would surely have switched it on again. And like so much radar, it would ping and bounce back to alert her to David's location.

Or it would have, except she wasn't receiving any signal.

Andra let out a huff of impatience and tried harder, extending her energy as far as she could, until it felt as if she were clamped to some terrible mental version of that old torture instrument known as "The Rack." She could feel tingling at the edges of her thought processes, a cerebral numbness threatening her physical form as her fingertips began to grow cold, followed by her forearms.

"What are you doing?" It was Margie's voice, though it sounded oddly slurred and far away, as if Andra were dreaming and Margie trying to wake her. Andra pressed her lips together hard and pushed on, though she was starting to feel dizzy with the exertion.

"Look now, you're turning blue!" Margie said, her tone scolding. "You stop that! Whatever you're doing, just stop it!"

Hands took hold of Andra's shoulders, roughly, and Andra felt her body go suddenly limp. She didn't even have the strength to lift her eyelids. She heard Margie say, "Well, come on and help me!" and then another set of hands were on her, the combined effort resulting in her being eased onto her back on the grass. It was cool, slightly damp, and Andra could feel it growing around and beneath her, could sense the myriad lifeforms moving through the blades and below the earth—a side effect of having extended her sensitivities so far. She would have happily napped there, but someone was shaking first one of her arms and then the other, alternating, the person's hands so warm as to feel near burning on Andra's cold skin.

"I mean, look at her!" Margie continued shrilly. "Blue!" And then, "Try slapping her cheeks. Oh, here, let me."

Andra opened her eyes then and rolled her head sideways just in time to avoid the blow. She found Walter standing over her, frowning down thoughtfully, while Margie knelt in the grass beside her, hand still up as if primed to take another swat.

"What was that all about?" Margie asked.

"I couldn't connect," said Andra, struggling to sit up. Walter offered her a hand.

"You've got some psychic tie to David, is that it?" asked Margie. Andra blinked at her, wondering how much to say and balancing that against how insane she might sound if she tried to explain. But Margie saved her at least half the trouble by going on quite reasonably, "David always was an odd one that way. Him and his mother, too, you know." She held up crossed fingers.

"You?" Andra asked.

Margie shook her head. "No, we never had it. I do wonder if it would have made a difference." Her lips twisted ruefully and she looked down at her hands for a brief moment before lifting her eyes and saying brightly, "But it was a good decade, anyway!"

Andra saw Walter transfer his frown to Margie, and Margie, seeming to feel it, turned to look up at him. "Even with the mother thing," she insisted.

"I hate his mother," Walter informed Margie flatly as he helped Andra the rest of the way to her feet. And as Andra struggled to steady herself—

Ping!

Suddenly Andra heard it, felt it tugging at her insides like so many tiny fishhooks attached to her soul. But what was she sensing? It wasn't the howling she'd heard before; this was instead eerily calm as it beckoned her. And as she turned away from the house to stare across the lawn, Andra felt an equal force attempting to warn her away. It pushed as the first pulled, a painful tug-of-war inside her as the hooks began to rip whatever psychic fabric they'd fastened onto. She had no choice but to follow the fishing line in hopes of slackening the aching.

"Are you all right?" she heard Walter ask, but Andra was already half stumbling across the grass, pausing only briefly to consider the thick black fog that seemed to be rolling in from offshore. There was something about it…

But she couldn't worry about that now. She had work to do. It was time to finish this job, one way or another.

INTERSTICE

"Care for a drink?"

Janus has been so focused on his mission he hadn't noticed the figure lurking beneath the trees that lined his path. "Bacchus," he says, drawing up short.

"I prefer Dionysus. More of a ring to it, less harsh." As Dionysus steps out onto the path and into the moonlight, Janus sees he's holding a cup. Not very unusual for him, of course. "Freshly squeezed," Dionysus says, "and you look thirsty."

But Janus ignores the proffered chalice. "Have you seen Hecate?"

"'Cate?" He withdraws the cup, studies its dark, liquid depths. "Maybe wine isn't what you're thirsty for after all."

"You call her 'Cate?"

Dionysus gives a small shrug calculated not to upset the contents of his drink. "Some of us are tighter knit than others." His eyes, black in the moonlight, note the way Janus stiffens and squares his body against the innuendo. "Is it blood or lust?" Dionysus wonders aloud. "Or a little of both?"

Janus grits his teeth. "She has something of mine."

"Blood it is." Dionysus' gaze drops again to his goblet. It is formed of fired clay with dancing red figures decorating a black background. "This was made by one of my most devoted craftsmen," he muses. "I would most certainly hate to lose it. But if it were for a good cause…" He lifts his gaze to where Janus stands, an older god, strong, his brow furrowed and stormy eyes roving—searching, Dionysus knows, for some sign of his quarry.

"Have a drink, Janus," Dionysus entreats. "You know I always have the best stuff."

"You haven't seen her?" Janus asks, even as he accepts the cup from Dionysus' hand.

"I didn't say that. It's a special blend," Dionysus adds as Janus takes a sip and makes a face.

"It's awful," says Janus.

"Well, I didn't make it for flavor," Dionysus admits. And as the cup falls from Janus' grasp, cracking open across a carefully painted satyr, Dionysus sighs, "I made it for a good cause."

14

"There's somebody out there," said Tina.

She and Liz stood on the patio, though Liz was looking longingly back at the doors; with the sun down, the breeze coming off the water had grown cool, and her eyelet summer dress no longer seemed like such a great idea.

"More than one somebody," Tina went on, and Liz finally turned to see what she was nattering about. Between where the light from the house ended and the distant lights of the garden began was nothing but blackness. But in that dark sea was the faint sense of something moving, shadows within shadows.

"It must be them," said Liz, starting across the flagstones and hoping movement would warm her up. "Come on."

But Tina hesitated, and as Liz paused to ask what the problem was, the patio door opened again and Mac and Craig emerged, and Liz's question became, "Did you find them?"

"Go back to your room, Liz. I can't have you catching a chill," said Mac.

Liz folded her arms across her body, as much to hold in

some body heat as to show Mac his concern was unwarranted. But before the argument could begin, Craig remarked, "There's somebody out there."

Mac cupped his hands around his mouth and used the full force of the voice he was so well known for. "Andra!"

"Andra? Who's Andra?" asked Liz. "We're looking for David."

"And Alfred," added Tina.

"Mac last saw Alfred with Andra, so…" Craig's voice trailed; he figured the less he said aloud the less likely it was anyone would start yelling at him. But when he saw the way Tina's face fell, he was sorry he'd said even that much.

"There's three of them all right," Mac said as two of the figures paused, one even offering something that might have been a wave, though none of them stopped walking. "Looks like they're headed toward the gardens."

"How can you even see that far?" Liz asked. "It's pitch black out there. Is this fog?"

"I have eyes like a cat," said Mac. He was already striding forward, and with only the briefest glance at Craig and Tina, Liz quickly followed suit, though she was immediately sorry when her heeled sandals sank into the damp grass.

Craig looked to Tina. She was driving her teeth into her lip, and her eyelashes were clumped with moisture that Craig knew had nothing to do with the night air. "You really like him," he said stupidly.

Tina's lips twisted up into a rueful smile. "They never last, though, do they? These on-set…" But Craig supposed she didn't have the heart to call it a "fling" or even an "affair" because Tina stopped then and made a little choking sound as if the letters had backed up in her throat.

Not sure where to look, Craig turned his eyes back to the lawn. He couldn't see Mac, but Liz's white dress was still visible and getting farther away by the second. If he and Tina were going to catch up, they'd need to get moving. He was just about to say as much to Tina when threads of darkness began to drift over Liz's disappearing figure, as if a great, dark hand were working to clutch her and lift her away. And even as Craig gave a tiny yelp of astonishment, Liz vanished from view altogether.

"Did you see that?" Craig asked.

"What?" Tina replied.

"The air just swallowed Liz."

"It's dark out there is all," said Tina. She started to step off the patio, but Craig put a staying hand on her arm.

"But just look," Craig insisted. "The lights of the garden, too. They're gone."

Tina hesitated then surprised Craig by drawing closer to him. "What's going on?" she asked. "What should we do?"

Craig straightened his shoulders. In the absence of the captain, it was the first mate's job to helm the ship. But first—

"We need flashlights," said Craig.

"How can you even see where you're going?" Margie asked.

"I'm not sure sight is what she's relying on," said Walter.

Andra didn't answer, only continued to plow ahead as she focused on the signal only she could hear.

Walter remained a half step behind her, seemingly content to let her lead, and Andra wondered how this all appeared to him. Could he simply chalk it up under crazy things actors did? Andra had seen her share of limelight insanity, and she was sure Walter had seen far more. But this wasn't a matter of alcoholism, drug addiction, or super ego; it wasn't a sex orgy or a secret gay lover—though as the thought crossed Andra's mind she almost stopped walking, even went so far as to glance back at Walter as if the truth might be easily read in the manager's features. But while Walter met her gaze steadily, his expression revealed nothing.

No, Andra decided. Even if David were gay, Alfred certainly wasn't. And with a further glance at the lagging Margie, Andra concluded it would have been a hell of a secret for David to keep for ten years.

"What?" Margie asked brightly when she caught Andra looking.

But Andra only shook her head. No, this wasn't the typical Hollywood (or whatever they had in England) tale of an actor's vices or quirks; it was, Andra thought, much, much weirder.

"Hi!" Margie suddenly called out, ostensibly to someone behind them, but Andra didn't bother to stop walking, and she noticed Walter kept pace as well. "Shouldn't we wait for them?" Margie asked.

"Actually, the fewer of us there are, the better, I think," said Walter, adding as Margie hesitated, "And you'd better keep up because it's getting darker."

AS DAVID CONTINUED to trail Alfred through the multi-tudinous paths, he thought the garden seemed far larger than it had the previous afternoon. "Where are we going?" he asked. "Or is this just a nice, nighttime stroll? Actors bonding and all that?"

Alfred didn't answer, but he didn't walk much farther either. They stopped in a kind of grassy circle that had paths extending from it in various directions, a crossroads made of lawn. "Just like always," Alfred sighed, then frowned slightly at the dark strands of fog that hovered above and around them, though it seemed to have cleared room for them where they stood, like an amorphous audience standing back from a stage. "Or not," he added thoughtfully.

David looked around at the substantive darkness. It seemed familiar, or was that only because he'd seen it in his nightmares? He recalled suddenly the way he'd pushed through the fog in his sleep; he'd been searching...

A visible *frisson* shook David, and Alfred said sympathetically, "It *is* a bit chilly tonight, isn't it?" Alfred reached into an interior pocket of his jacket, and for a terrible second David had the idea his co-star was reaching for a gun. But the item that flashed in Alfred's hand was not so deadly; it was merely a flask, an old one by the look of it.

David relaxed. "Wrap party gift?" he asked as he eyed the etched silver that had been rubbed smooth in places from years of regular handling.

"Older than that," Alfred remarked. He unscrewed the flask's cap. "This vintage, too, is old. Good for warming up on a night like this."

"It's not really that cold out," said David. "It's summer, after all." But he found himself holding out his hand for the flask all the same.

"But we're out here by the water," Alfred said. "And the breeze is getting stronger, I think. No, Davey darling, not for you," he added and reached again into his jacket, this time producing the dog-eared paperback. "Come on out, Janus. Have a drink for old times' sake."

"OKAY, MISTER CAT EYES," Liz grumbled as she stumbled, not for the first time; the lawn had seemed much flatter in the light of day. "Where are we going? I don't see anyone out here."

Mac kept walking. "Some kind of fog," he muttered.

"Hold my hand," said Liz, grabbing Mac's without waiting for permission.

"What? No!" Mac tried to shake her off, but Liz tightened her grip, even as she bent to adjust her sandal strap with her free hand, forcing Mac to a standstill.

"If we don't hold hands, we're just going to end up separated and lost," Liz said. "And do you really need any more wandering sheep?"

"Oh, for Christ's sake." But Mac didn't attempt to disengage her again. Instead, he yanked her back up to standing. "Speaking of which…" He craned to look right then left.

Liz finished his thought. "Where are Craig and Tina?"

TINA HAD KNOWN EXACTLY where Lighting kept their stores, and it had taken them no time at all to find and appropriate what they needed, though Craig made a mental note to send a memo reminding the Lighting crew to lock up the equipment after hours.

Once they'd returned to the patio, they walked to the very edge of the light where the estate's illumination stretched from its windows and outdoor lamps, to where it fell almost abruptly into darkness, a seeming cliff of black void. Craig knew, of course, that there was grass out there. Just grass. And that the apparent emptiness was nothing more than a trick of the light, or lack of it. But he still found himself reluctant to take that next step, and from the way Tina stood beside him, her feet close together and toes just shy of the shadows, he had an idea she felt the same.

Still, Craig switched on his industrial-grade flashlight (or as Tina, being British, had corrected him, "torch") and Tina followed suit. The rays of light cut into what appeared to be a wall of darkness, black as a starless night sky. And yet the flashlights didn't penetrate that darkness; instead, the beams were absorbed into it.

"I don't get it," said Tina.

Craig just shook his head. "Well, we can't leave them in there." He glanced at Tina to see if she was game, watched her set her mouth with forced resolve. Then she nodded.

"Okay."

"Stay close to me," Craig instructed, and Tina nodded again.

Craig stepped forward into the dark.

"I PROMISED HER, YOU SEE," Alfred explained as David's gaze narrowed in on the book and grew increasingly dark. "Or maybe I promised myself. It's been so long, it gets difficult to remember."

"Why?" asked David. Or what looked like David, had been him minutes before.

"It's so much more fun here," said Alfred. "And anyway, 'Cate's made good use of the key at least. Would you go around helping people realize their dreams, opening the gates of destiny? Or whatever it is she does."

"It's mine," said David.

"It's mine," mimicked Alfred. "Jesus, you sound like a child. Can't you share your toys?"

"She's had a turn with it for three thousand years."

"Well, there is that," Alfred conceded. He eyed the man before him thoughtfully then held out the flask. "Look, why don't you have a drink and we can discuss the options."

But before David could accept the offer, the dark clouds around them began to boil and billow in a kind of angry frustration, as if something were caught behind them and was trying to push its way out.

"What…?" Alfred began as the fog collected into a dense pillar and finally resolved itself in the shape of a woman: middle-aged, statuesque, and dressed in shimmering peacock blue.

"Don't you dare," she said, though it wasn't clear if she was speaking to Alfred or David. In any case, Alfred took a step back to reassess the situation while David blinked with incomprehension.

"Mum?"

15

"Speak of the devil, and the devil appears," said Walter.

They'd been traversing the paths of the garden, moving swiftly through its turns as Andra continued to follow her internal beacon while attempting to ignore the equally insistent signal ordering her away. The push-pull was something she'd never encountered before, and the dissonance required Andra to focus in even more intently if she were going to find the sources. Both signals were originating in the same vicinity, if not from the same person.

As they had rounded a stand of tall rosebushes filled with pink and white blooms, they'd heard voices, and Margie had given a squeak and rushed ahead, only to stop short when the air around them began to move.

Andra had hardly noticed the dark fog that had enveloped the estate grounds; her focus had been on following the signal, which had never steered her wrong, and for which the darkness was not an issue. So she was surprised to see the black clouds draw up and away, funneling in the direction they were moving. With Walter on her heels, Andra had hurried to where Margie stood peering around the last of the rosebushes. The fog was gone; a woman stood in the clearing with Alfred and David. And that was when Walter had uttered the old adage.

"What do you mean?" Andra asked him.

"That's David's mother," Margie answered grimly.

"The fog was his mother?" Andra asked. Could the night get any stranger?

"Always knew she was a witch," muttered Walter.

"I may be old, but my hearing is perfect," the woman called. "So you might as well come out and join us. Ah, Walter and Marjorie, how lovely," she said, making it sound like anything but lovely as the trio approached.

All at once Andra realized David and Alfred had been the sources of the signals, with David pulling and Alfred pushing. Though as she stepped into the clearing, the pushing stopped and Alfred gave up, asking, "Don't you have enough sense to run the other way?"

The tugging on her insides continued, however. Yet as Andra turned to David—did he even know he was hurting her? did he mean to?—she encountered instead the pale blue eyes of his mother. They sent a chill through Andra. The eyes were so like David's but much, much colder.

"And Trivia," David's mother added, the words falling flat like a thud.

"Hecate," David corrected under his breath.

"What's that?" his mother asked sharply, though there was no question she'd heard, and as she turned to look at her son, he didn't speak again. Her gaze crawled over him a moment longer before returning to Andra and settling on the chain around her neck. "Hand it over."

LIZ'S HAND tightened on Mac's as the cloud surrounding them began to swirl and move. "Mac?"

"It's fine," said Mac, using his best director voice.

"What if it's a tornado?"

"There's no wind," he pointed out, and at that moment the seemingly manufactured darkness lifted and funneled away from them. "Where's it going?" Mac wondered, automatically turning his steps to follow.

Liz tugged on his arm. "Then we should go the other way," she said.

Before Mac could answer, voices began to hail them from behind. In tacit agreement, Liz and Mac released each other's hands and turned to find Tina and Craig jogging in their direction, each carrying an industrial-grade flashlight. The beam of Craig's landed square in Mac's eyes, and Mac slapped the device aside. "Would you put that down?"

Craig obediently lowered his flashlight, and Tina turned hers off. "Weird weather," she said.

"Footprints," Craig added with an air of pride. He pointed the beam of light at the grass in front of his feet, illuminating grass that had been clearly mussed by traffic, particularly the divots of a pair of high heels. "We found them and were following them. You, really. We were following you. Your footprints. To get to you. Both of you, I mean." Craig was becoming aware that the more he kept talking, the more pronounced Mac's frown became, so he stopped and threw Liz a plaintive look.

"Good job, Scooby," Liz offered, and Craig brightened.

"Right, well, now that we're not lost any more, let's find the ones who are," said Mac. "And I suggest we start over there." He pointed in the direction the dark cloud had traveled.

Liz balked. "What makes you think they're over there?"

"What makes you think they're not?" Mac countered.

Craig shined his torch over the grass, angling to stretch

the beam of light. "I think he's right," he said when he found signs of more footprints farther on.

"The director's always right, is that it?" asked Liz.

"Whether he's right or not, he's the director," said Craig. "It's his job, after all. His whole reason for being."

For a long moment the other three just started at him. Craig met their eyes, each in turn, then dropped his gaze to his shoes and mumbled, "I think about these things sometimes."

"Clearly," said Mac, and after another moment, "Lead on, then."

Craig's head shot up.

"You're the one with the flashlight," Mac insisted. "Go on and direct."

Craig glanced uncertainly at Liz. She didn't look happy, but she managed to quirk up a corner of her mouth in a half smile for his sake. "Earn that Scooby snack," she prompted. "But I'm going to blame you if I get eaten by a tornado. That's all I'm saying."

"Right. Okay," said Craig, too nervous to ask Liz what she meant. "Well then, if you'll just follow me..."

"It's not a tour, Craig," Mac said, and was startled when Liz put a hand on his arm.

"Let him have this one," she whispered.

Mac peered thoughtfully at her. "Do I detect a heart in there after all?"

"Oh, see, definitely three people," Craig was saying as he swung his light in an arc in front of him. Tina had turned hers back on as backup, was walking with Craig as Mac and Liz fell a little behind.

Liz shrugged. "An actress has many hearts, though only one is her own."

"That's from *Dreams of a Tap Dancer*," said Mac, "only in the movie you say 'dancer' instead of 'actress.'"

Liz looked up in surprise. "You saw that? No one saw that. Not even me; I snuck out the back at the premiere."

"It was pretty bad," Mac conceded.

"Thanks a lot."

"Blame the director," suggested Mac.

"It was the script that was lousy," Liz said.

"Oh, wait," Craig was saying from some distance ahead of them. "These are two different sets of footprints." Beside him, Tina dutifully stopped to join her light with his.

"We should put a leash on him," said Mac.

"Oh, just let him run. This must be the best night of his life."

"I've had worse," Mac admitted, and when Liz glanced up at him, "Not weirder. But worse."

"We could follow these or…" Craig was turning in a small circle. He paused to wait for Liz and Mac to join them, turning his wide eyes on the director as if looking for instruction.

"Don't look at me," said Mac. "This is what directing is all about."

"I think they were headed for the garden," Tina said.

Craig looked from Mac to Tina to the ground, made a decision, and set off again with Tina right behind him.

"I wish I at least had a stick to throw for him," said Mac, and Liz's laughter pealed over the quiet night air.

"PERHAPS SOME INTRODUCTIONS FIRST," Alfred proposed. "'Cate, this is Hera."

"Juno," David's mother corrected. "And I already know everyone here, so let's get down to brass tacks, as it were. The key."

"Oh my God, you're Alfred Keenan," Margie said suddenly, "I just loved you in *Breaking Midnight*."

Everyone stopped to stare, first at Margie and then at Alfred, who spared a precious moment to preen. Andra gestured at the flask. "What's that?"

"Some refreshment for Janus here. He's very tired and thirsty from chasing you around." Alfred stretched the flask nearer to David, but David's dark gaze was now riveted to Andra.

"Janus?" Margie asked.

"An old Greek god," Walter answered. "Had two faces, guarded gateways. And Juno…"

"Yes, Juno," that goddess said impatiently, "is still waiting. I've come to do what my son has been unable or unwilling to do for the past three thousand years. Never send a boy to do a woman's job."

Andra only half heard the conversation going on around her, for the fishing line inside her was being pulled in earnest now, and all at once she realized she was the fish, caught and wriggling and helpless as it reeled her in. And even though David—Janus—merely continued to stand there and stare at her, the very will in his gaze had her stepping forward.

"'Cate," Alfred warned, halting Andra's progress. But her attention remained on David.

"Why do you want it?" she asked. "What use can it possibly be to you?"

David still did not move or speak, and after a moment Juno snapped, "It's the key to Olympus, girl. None of us can get home without it."

Andra's brow furrowed as she tried to make sense of this information, and though it took effort, she managed to tear her eyes from David and refocus them on Alfred in silent search of confirmation, an explanation, anything that might help.

"I like it here," Alfred said with a small shrug. "And you've never seemed to have much desire to leave, either."

He gave the flask a little shake as if to entice David the way one might tempt a cat with a toy. "Have a drink. You'll feel better."

David's gaze turned toward the shining silver offering, but his mother prevented any attempt he might have made to accept it by saying, "No, Janus, you don't want that."

Andra watched the way David's lips pulled downward into a deep frown then turned back to Juno. "What will you do with it? If I give it to you? I mean, doesn't it belong to David? Or Janus, that is?" Her gaze returned to David, and his dark eyes met hers, but she couldn't read them, couldn't make anything of his expression.

"Okay," said Alfred in a voice meant for the stage, "you two then. A drink?" He transferred the flask from his left hand to his right and held it out for Walter and Margie. "Just be sure to save some for everyone else."

Margie stepped forward, beaming; Walter stayed where he was. As he handed Margie the flask, Alfred remarked, "You would look quite lovely with a crown of ivy in your hair."

"Bacchus," Walter said with sudden understanding.

"Dionysus, rather," Alfred corrected smoothly. He winked at Margie and she giggled. "It's a very special brew."

Walter came forward then. "Don't drink it."

Margie bit her lip, glanced at Andra and David, but they had eyes only for one another. Neither Walter nor Alfred failed to notice the swift expression of hurt that swept across Margie's features, though it was almost instantly replaced with her usual, if forced, cheerfulness. She grinned first at Walter, then Alfred.

"It will make you forget," Alfred told her gently, and Margie's smile slipped slightly.

"How much?"

Alfred's shoulders sagged. "Truthfully, I don't know. I've never tried it on a pure mortal before."

"Don't drink it," Walter said again.

"And what will you do?" Alfred asked him. "Go out and tell the world Greek gods are hiding in human form?"

But Walter responded with a quelling look. "I work with people who think they're gods every day. It's immaterial to me whether they really are or not."

"Speaking of which," said Alfred. He turned to where Andra and David appeared locked in a kind of stasis. "They do this every time," he sighed, then called, "'Cate! If you give him the key to unlock Olympus, David will cease to exist. So if you're truly here to help him, I'm not sure that counts."

"I DON'T REMEMBER the garden being this big," Mac remarked as he and Liz continued to follow Craig and Tina through the myriad pathways.

"Were the plants always this tall?" Liz wondered aloud. Some of the hedges and rosebushes were several inches above her head.

"Maybe they look shorter from the house. Distance, perspective," said Mac.

Liz gave him a friendly nudge. "Thinking like a director."

"Always," said Mac.

Ahead of them, Craig turned in another little circle like a hound looking for a scent. Tina stopped beside him for a short consultation, and Liz put a staying hand on Mac's arm. "Give them a minute."

Mac frowned down at her—but not too far down, since he wasn't much taller. "What? Why?"

"She's stuck on Alfred."

"That's no good," Mac put in.

"But maybe…" Liz gave a nod toward where Craig and Tina stood shoulder to shoulder, deep in discussion, gesturing with their flashlights.

"Cute," said Mac, "you're a matchmaker."

Liz smiled up at him. "You think I'm cute?" she teased.

"What? No! I mean, that's not—"

Liz's grin widened. "I don't think I've ever seen you flustered."

"I don't get flustered," Mac told her.

"Oh, but you did just then."

"That wasn't flustered, that was you—"

But Craig and Tina were calling and waving them on.

"We should go find the others," said Liz, though reluctance edged her tone.

"Yeah," Mac agreed, no less resigned.

"David," said Liz.

"And Andra," said Mac.

But there was a drag in their steps as they moved to join their bloodhounds. And if their hands brushed now and again, neither of them drew back.

16

Andra looked from David to Juno to Alfred and back again. David—or Janus, she supposed—appeared remarkably unmoved by Alfred's declaration. And Alfred merely arched a brow.

But it was Margie who demanded, "What do you mean, he'll cease to exist?"

"If Janus opens the gates of Olympus, our mortal forms will be unable to remain intact," said Alfred. "We've been away from home too long and no longer have the power to hold these bodies together." He turned a piercing look on David. "Which wouldn't put Janus or his mother out in the least, but as I said, I've been enjoying myself and rather like it here."

Andra reached for the necklace clasp at her nape. "It was never David who was calling to me," she said. "It was Janus all along. _He's_ the one I was meant to help." She slipped the key from the chain and held it out to David. "Take it."

The dark eyes darted to the key in the outstretched palm.

"This is what I do," Andra insisted. "I go where I'm

called. If you're sad because you're locked in that body…"
She jiggled the key as if to coax David into taking it.

"Do they always do this too?" Walter asked.

"No," said Alfred slowly, "this bit is new. But then again, *he* usually finds *her* and not the other way around. Tricky, two-faced bastard. He's learning. Only took him thirty-some-odd lifetimes. 'Cate, darling," he called to Andra, "he's preying on your good intentions. He called you here because he knew you wouldn't be able to refuse, and it was easier than continuing to chase you. Lazy sod."

But it was Juno who moved. She strode to where Andra stood and snatched the key from her palm then went and slapped it into her son's palm. "Go on then. Or will I have to do this for you, too?"

David stared for a minute at the key in his hand. Then he looked at his mother, then back at Andra.

"What's he supposed to do?" Margie asked.

"He has to swallow it, sweetheart," Alfred explained. "Like Alice in Wonderland. Eat me or…" He brandished the flask. "Drink me."

"WE CAN HEAR THEM," Craig explained as Mac and Liz joined him and Tina beside a remarkably tall stand of roses. They all paused to listen to the distinct carry of voices coming over the wall of green.

Tina swept her light down the seemingly unending stretch of rosebushes. "It's like a fairy tale, you know? *Briar Rose?*" she said.

"Oh, I was in that movie; I played Lady in Waiting Number Two," said Liz, earning a strange look from the makeup artist.

"Well, if there's no way around, I guess we'll have to go through," said Mac.

"Roses have thorns," Craig said, and sent his own flashlight beam onto the bushes to prove his point. The light touched on the long, sharp defenses of the flowers.

"Beautiful but painful," Liz mused.

"What, like you?" Mac asked, and when Liz's jaw dropped and her eyes flashed, he smiled. "Now who's flustered?"

"I'm not flustered," Liz informed him, her voice strangled, "I'm—"

But Mac was taking the flashlight from Craig. "Don't worry, Craig, I'll take over from here." And he pushed into the briars.

"WHAT HAPPENS IF HE DRINKS THAT?" Margie asked.

"He forgets," said Alfred in a low voice, his attention fixed on David. "Same as always."

"And her?" Walter asked with a nod at Andra.

Alfred spared him a glance. "'Cate?"

"Katie?"

"Hecate," Alfred elaborated as he went back to eyeing David and Andra with interest. "She has her own thing."

"And this happens often?" Walter went on.

"Every century or so. Though Juno isn't usually on hand." He looked appraisingly at the small, grey-haired man in the thick specs and said, "You're taking this remarkably well."

Walter shrugged. "You see all kinds of shit in this business. Be a shame to lose him, though. He had a good career ahead of him."

"The hell he did."

All heads swung toward a stretch of nearby rosebushes as Mac came plunging through, swearing as the thorns attacked his clothes and any exposed skin. "Whatever you've done to Andra, David—"

"He hasn't done anything to me," Andra said.

But Mac had spotted the key in David's hand. "That's your key."

"Mac," Andra began.

"You never go anywhere without it," Mac went on, his voice beginning to rise. "What did he do, steal it?"

"Rather the other way around," muttered Alfred.

"And what's your part in this, Keenan?" Mac demanded.

"Just offering refreshments," Alfred replied undauntedly, swinging the flask in Mac's direction. "Care for any?"

Behind Mac, the rosebush shuddered once more only to reveal Liz, her eyelet sundress somewhat the worse for wear after having been clawed by the plant. "David!" she said, stopping short when faced with Juno's imperious stare.

"I'm not going to have enough to go around at this rate," said Alfred.

David tilted his hand so the key slid to his fingertips then began to twist it thoughtfully between his thumb and forefinger, causing it to twirl. He looked again to Andra, watched the bright yellow shoot across her irises like wishing stars. "I wasn't hallucinating," he said, the words thick and slow. "They really do that."

Andra's brow puckered and she turned to Alfred. "Your eyes, love," he told her. "We all have them."

When Andra leaned in as if to look into his eyes, Alfred drew back, but not before she saw what he meant. She opened her mouth to mention it, but Alfred cut her short with a wink and a tiny shake of his head.

"If you have an issue with my client," Walter was saying to Mac.

"Swallow it," Juno instructed her son. "I'm sick of the confines of these mortal coils. Let's go home." But this time David did not so much as look at her, all his attention on Andra.

Margie, meanwhile, saw where David's interest lay. He'd

looked at her once and only once, and she was beginning to understand he wasn't going to look her way again. So she marched back to Alfred, swiped the flask from his hand, and took a good swallow. She might've drunk more, but one swig was all she could choke down.

"God, it's awful!" Margie sputtered.

"It's what they all say," Alfred sighed, gently relieving her of the flask.

"I thought you were the god of wine," said Walter.

"What the fuck are you talking about?" asked Mac.

"Not every vintage is a winner," said Alfred, his lips set in a thin, grim line. He slid an arm around Margie's waist.

"Hey," she protested, but not too vehemently.

"What god of wine?" Mac insisted. He looked to Andra. "Is this to do with your thing?" And then gesturing to Juno, "And who is she?"

Margie stepped backward into Alfred's supporting arm, and her left knee gave out from under her, causing her to slide. "Oopsie," Alfred said. He handed Andra the flask, thus freeing himself to ease Margie onto the grass.

David moved then, directly for Andra. From where he knelt beside Margie, Alfred tensed like a cat ready to pounce, and even Walter appeared ready to intervene. But Mac was the one to step between David and his quarry.

"Oh no you don't."

"Janus!" Juno snapped.

"Who's Janus?" asked Liz, coming to stand beside Mac.

"Mac, really, it's fine," said Andra. She stepped around her would-be protector and said to David, "You have what you want."

"And what do *you* want?" David asked.

The question threw Andra; no one had ever bothered to ask her before, nor had she dared to ask herself. "To do my job," she finally told him, though she sounded uncertain in her own ears. "Just like you. Well, like David. I don't know *you*, what you…"

"Hecate," David said, and then as if trying it out to see if he could get away with it, "'Cate."

"It's Andra. Really. I mean, I know Alfred is all integrated or whatever, but I just… I don't feel like anyone other than me."

"That's what integration is, darling," Alfred said. "It's all you, accepting and living with your human form. But Janus here refuses to play nice with his hosts. Threw the last one in the Thames. I really don't know what's going to happen this one," he added, putting a couple fingers on Margie's wrist to take a pulse. "It's one thing when you've got a deity inside you, something else again when you don't."

"Would someone please tell me what the fuck is going on?" Mac cried.

CRAIG AND TINA hovered on the other side of the roses, neither one quite ready or willing to take the plunge.

"How thick do you think they are?" Craig asked, and Tina shook her head.

"No way to tell, really." She held up the remaining flashlight and attempted to shine it through the thick, glossy leaves, but there was nothing but a dark tangle.

"You don't think they got caught in there?" Craig ventured.

"What, like in the fairy tale?" asked Tina. And after some consideration, "No, of course not. We'd hear something." But she didn't sound all that certain.

Stopping to listen, they could hear the voices on the other side of the roses, but the words were indistinct, and no one voice could be easily identified.

They stood there a moment longer. Then Craig took a deep breath and said, "Well, when the director isn't here…"

"We could see if there's a way around," Tina suggested. Once again she moved the beam down the length of greenery, but there were no apparent cracks or breaks in the foliage.

Craig shook his head. "You can if you want, but I've got to do this." When Tina attempted to hand him the light, Craig held up a hand. "No. I'll be fine without it." He reached for what appeared the most likely spot for entering the hedge, a place where two thick boughs curved in a way to suggest a kind of hole; Craig thought he might be able to push them apart and squeeze in. "Just wish I had some gloves."

Tina turned the flashlight off and set it on the ground. Craig glanced back at her. "What are you doing?"

"You wouldn't leave me out here alone, would you?" Tina asked, but before Craig could answer, she went on, "Well, I'm not letting you go in there alone either."

They locked eyes, and Craig nodded. He opened the bush as best he could and sidled in sideways, holding branches back for Tina the way a gentleman might hold a door—a very thorny, hateful door. She slipped in behind him, and as the briars snapped closed behind her, Tina grabbed the hem of Craig's shirt.

"Dark in here," she breathed.

"Maybe we should've brought the, er, torch after all," said Craig. "Guess I'm not so good at this." He continued to push sideways into the brambles, Tina following his small, crablike steps.

"You're great at it," she told him.

Craig paused. "Yeah?"

"Yeah. But you have to keep moving forward if you're going to get anywhere."

"Right," said Craig, and he began to forge ahead once more, hands up in front of his face to brave off any thorns that might aim for his eyes. Yet, remarkably, the only pull he felt came from Tina hanging on his shirttail. "I see light," he said a minute later, and they broke through to the clearing and stepped out of the roses in a shower of pink and white petals, though no one seemed to notice their arrival.

Just in front of them, his back to them, was David's manager Walter. Not far from him knelt Alfred beside a strange blond woman. And there were Andra and David, staring into one another, not seeming to notice at all that Mac was working desperately to wedge himself between them. Liz stood next to Mac. And in front of David stood a matronly figure in a peacock blue gown, glowering at David in a way that made Craig understand immediately she was David's mother, because only a mother could adopt a look of such utter disapproval.

"If I drink it?" David asked Alfred, never turning his eyes from Andra.

"You'll go to sleep for another hundred years, give or take. Janus, I mean. And poor David Styles won't know what hit him."

Now David did look at Alfred. "He won't remember?"

Alfred darted a look at Andra. "They don't usually, no."

"You're not going to drink it," said Juno. "You're going to swallow that key."

David looked at his mother. "No, Mum, I've told you before. I'm really not."

David turned back to Andra, pressed the key into her palm and took the flask from her other hand. "To another hundred years then. Cheers."

"WHAT...?" Craig began in a whisper; he felt like he'd walked in on a play being performed, and that he shouldn't interrupt or distract the players. Tina only shook her head to indicate she didn't know. Her eyes were on Alfred, who was kneeling in the grass beside a curvy blond woman who seemed to have passed out on the lawn.

"That's the worst thing I've ever tasted," David said. He pressed the back of his hand to his mouth. "Good God, Alfred, you really will drink anything, won't you? Margie?" he said then as his eyes fell his ex-girlfriend. "What's she doing here? And Mum?"

"I don't know what's going on," said Mac. "But as the director, I insist—" But he stopped short when Liz placed a hand on his arm and gave her head a little shake.

"Is she all right?" David asked, gesturing at Margie's prone figure.

Alfred leaned over Margie, head tilted as if to listen, either for a heartbeat or breath. "No, I'm afraid she might not be."

"How much do you remember?" Andra asked David, and he swung his frown in her direction.

"I thought you were supposed to leave once the house was empty," he said.

Andra bit her lip and looked away from David only to find Juno's blizzardly gaze drilling into her. "You will give me that key," Juno told her.

Reflexively, Andra's hand closed around the ancient bronze artifact.

"You can give it to her if you want," Alfred told Andra, "but short of shoving it down her son's throat, it won't do her any good."

Juno scowled at him over her shoulder. "I never have liked you, Bacchus. You're a troublemaker and an instigator. Always have been."

"Mum?" David asked, following her gaze and clearly trying to figure out what feud she might have with his co-star.

"Janus is the god of gates," Alfred explained to Andra, ignoring Juno's fangless bite and David's confusion. "You may be able to do much with that key, but he's the only one with the power to open Olympus."

Andra opened her hand again. "And I..."

"Stole it," Juno told her. "And my son has spent millennia trying to get it back." She took in David's blank expression and sighed. "Maybe if I baked it into a cake."

Walter joined Alfred, kneeling on the other side of Margie's prone figure. "She's got a pulse at least," said Walter. "Let's get her up and to the house. On three." He counted and they hauled Margie's dead weight to standing, then Alfred swung her form fully into his arms to allow him to carry her. Margie's blond head lolled against Alfred's shoulder.

"Let's go," Tina whispered to Craig.

"Shouldn't we see if they need any help?" Craig asked.

"Please, Craig." She gave his hand a tug. "Let's just go."

"What, back through the roses?"

Alfred, too, had found himself temporarily stymied when confronted by the wall of thorns and blooms. "'Cate, if you would?" he called.

"Would what?" Andra asked.

"Goddess of crossroads, holding the key," Alfred incanted, shifting Margie's weight in his arms. "I mean, she's lovely and all, but not light, so if you could..."

"I don't—" Andra began, but the key in her hand began to feel warm, the heat running up her arm and into her head and chest so that she felt fuzzy inside. And at Alfred's feet the roses parted and a grassy path appeared.

"Thank you, darling. Always is a treat to see you at your work," said Alfred, and he set off for the house, Walter in his wake.

· · ·

CRAIG STOPPED to pick up the flashlight they'd left on the other side of the roses. "We should take this back to Lighting."

He and Tina had waited a minute to let Alfred and Walter get some distance before slipping away on the same path. If anyone had seen them, had even realized they'd been there, they hadn't said anything. Now Tina stood watching the shadowy figures climb the sloping lawn to the house. Alfred reached the light of the patio, and Tina could see the long blond hair trailing over Alfred's arm. She turned away.

"Weird stuff, huh?" Craig asked. He glanced back through the hole in the rosebush, then up at where Walter was holding the door so Alfred could get Margie into the house, and finally down at the light in his hand. "Guess we don't need this now, either."

Tina reached for it. "I'll put it back."

"No, it's okay, I'll—Oh, hey!" Craig yelped as Tina's tears let loose. "No, okay, if you really want to put it back."

"He didn't even notice me," said Tina.

"Well, you know, he kind of had his hands f— Wait, no, that's not the right thing..." Craig began glancing around in earnest, looking for help.

Tina stifled a sniffle. "No, it's okay, really. I'm okay. I just... I went looking for him, and..."

"Well, I guess I'm used to it," said Craig. "Being over-looked, I mean."

"I should have known better than to go looking for someone who stood me up," Tina went on. "It's like what they say about listening at doors. Never hearing anything good about oneself." When Craig only looked bewildered, Tina explained, "If you go looking for someone who's stood you up, you probably won't like what you find. That's all."

"Or maybe," Craig suggested, working to salvage the situation and hopefully prevent more tears, "you find something different. That might be just as good? Oh, here," he said, pulling a handkerchief from his pocket and offering it to Tina.

"You carry a handkerchief?" she asked as she accepted it; a quick inspection found it to be remarkably clean besides.

Craig shrugged. "My mom, you know. She believes a proper young man carries a handkerchief."

Tina smiled in spite of herself. "Can I keep it? Just long enough to wash it for you."

"Sure. I mean, I've got loads of them," said Craig.

They stood there in awkward silence for a moment.

"So, I'll just…" Craig waggled the flashlight.

"I'll come with you," said Tina. "To make sure you put it in the right place. Else Eddie will know, and he's very particular."

Craig glanced back again through the roses. "Mac has the other one."

"He and Eddie can sort that out between them tomorrow. But for tonight…"

Craig nodded. "For tonight, it's up to me. At least on this end." He looked again through the opening in the rosebush; he could see Andra's back, and Mac's shoulder, the top of David's head, the hem of David's mother's dress.

Tina startled Craig by taking hold of his arm. "Come on, then, Director. This isn't our scene."

"ANDRA," Mac said.

"David," said Liz.

"Mum, what are you doing here?" David asked.

Juno looked up at her son. "Trying to get you to do the one thing you're on this earth to do. For all the good it's done me."

"I don't understand," said David.

"No, you wouldn't, would you? And you won't for at least

another hundred years." Juno rounded on Andra. "Hand it here." She held out her palm.

Andra instinctively took a step back, and Mac closed rank beside her. "Your son's career is over if you lay a single finger on Andra or her key."

Juno snorted. "Do you honestly think I'm worried about his acting career? I'm trying to get home. And once that gate is open, there will be no David Styles in any case."

"I won't swallow it, Mum. Regardless of what you do or say."

All eyes swung toward David. Andra peered hard into the famous face—well, semi-famous, anyway—and saw the blue of the irises shifting from light to dark and back, as if someone were attempting to adjust a light.

"You didn't drink it," she realized.

"Maybe you have some sense after all," his mother added. "Now let's go home." She waved her fingers at Andra in a "gimmie" gesture.

"Not if 'Cate—Andra—doesn't want to," said David.

"You must be joking," said Juno, turning her hard stare back to Andra for a second before telling her son, "It's your key by rights."

"And I'm giving it to her," David said.

"Well, now that that's settled," said Mac. "We can—"

"You can't," Juno told David. "It's your duty to open that gate and get us home."

"And what would you do there?" David asked. "Stride around Olympus complaining about Jove? 'Cate at least has a true purpose. She uses that key to help people. I'm not going to stop her, not unless she asks me to."

Juno rounded on Andra once more. "Give it to him then. Tell him you want to go home like the rest of us."

Andra tried to conjure up some image, some feeling for the mythical Olympus but came up blank. "This *is* home.

Here. Well, New Orleans, but anyway, not Olympus. I don't have any memory of it. And I like being a K-Pro." She turned pleading eyes to David. "I'm sorry. I know it's disappointing."

"I'm not disappointed," David assured her. "And Olympus is probably filled with cobwebs by now." He looked at his mother. "We're not the big shots we once were."

"Vesta will have kept it tidy," said Juno roundly.

"You could still be a big shot here," Liz put in. "Movie star and all. So long as you don't set Mac off." She nodded to where the director was standing, arms folded and eyes riveted, as if watching a take.

David sighed. "I'll always take care of you, Mum. Even get you put in a movie if you like. But this is one thing I can't do for you. Not this time around."

Juno drew away from her son, turned and walked away several steps. Andra saw in David's face how it hurt him to think he'd upset his mother. She realized then, too, that she could hear the crying in him again, and Andra opened her hand, prepared to give up the key, have David swallow it, if that would relieve the lines of suffering she read on his face, if it would staunch the tears inside him.

But then Juno turned to regard her son from over her shoulder, her lips twisting in a way both sly and grudging. "What kind of movie?" she asked.

David smiled and Andra's heart skipped a little; she hadn't seen him smile once since she arrived, except when the script called for it. "Mac?" David asked, "What kind of part do you have for my mother?"

"What?" Mac asked, startled out of whatever thoughts he'd been having. He looked from David to Andra, then past them to Juno. "Well, we could..."He looked at Andra again. "You'll be staying on set for a while?"

Andra glanced at David. "I think I'm finished here," she said uncertainly.

"Give us a minute," David said. "Find Mum a room and a role and—"

"Hold on a second," Mac put in, "*I'm* the director, and *I'll* —" He stopped as Andra bit her lip and turned her big green eyes on him. "...Find your mother a room and a role," he finished, holding an elbow out for Juno to take so that he could escort her back to the house.

As Mac turned away, Liz hugged herself and pressed her lips together, seemingly forgotten and abandoned. But then Mac moved to hold out his other hand, only to discover he was still holding an industrial torch. "Huh." So he extended his other elbow instead. "Come along, Ms. Hellmann. This is our cue to exit."

But Liz held up a finger in indication that he should wait. She strode the few steps to David and planted herself in front him, hands on her hips. "Let me just say: I put this dress on for you," she said, "and went out looking for you in a dark fog, nearly got lost, pushed through Jurassic-sized rose-bushes—" And here she displayed a well-scratched forearm, "for you, and I don't know what all this is about—" Her finger described a wide circle in the air, "but I sincerely hope I never, *ever* work with you again!" And with that, Liz whirled on her much muddied heeled sandals and took firm hold of Mac's proffered elbow, half towing him even as Juno marched along on his other arm.

"Poor Mac," Andra sighed as she and David watched them go. "He's going to want an explanation, and I'm not sure I have one."

David held up the silver flask. "Just give him some of this."

But that only served to remind Andra. "Margie."

"Alfred will look after her."

Andra chewed her lip for a while longer. Then, "Why didn't you drink it?"

"Have you tasted it? It's awful." But as the bright green eyes searched his face, he admitted, "I didn't want to forget you."

Andra looked hard at him. David's eyes had settled into their bright blue, but they now featured a darker ring of color around the pupil and again at the outer edge of the irises. "You're integrating."

"When you can't beat them…" After another long pause, he asked, "You'll stay?"

Andra felt her heart tighten inside her chest. "I shouldn't. I don't usually. Seeing Mac again has reminded me of all the reasons I don't see clients after… And anyway, I'm always on call. So I never stay anywhere very long. Even if I want to."

"Do you want to?"

"What I want doesn't matter," Andra insisted. "My job, my life, is about doing for others."

"Well, what about me then?" David asked.

Andra felt a flutter of panic in her throat. But she had to do this right. "What do you want?" she asked.

"I want you."

"Well that's… I mean…" Was that even allowed? She didn't know. So she went with what she did know and asked the next question. "Are you sure?"

"More sure of that than anything in this world. I've loved you for three thousand years, 'Cate. All I ever wanted was to take you home. Because I thought you'd be happier away from all the crying hearts of this world. But if this is what you want, what you value… Just don't keep running away. Tell me that no matter where your work takes you, you'll always come back to me."

And just like that, Andra felt her heart loosen and her fears ebb away. Maybe by granting his wish she could fulfill her own. It was worth a try at least.

"Yes," she said. "I can do that. I can promise you that."

EPILOGUE

He wakes, momentarily confused. He does not know who or where he is, only that his body feels too heavy, his mouth too dry.

Dawn is coming over the hills, Aurora at her work. The sunlight warms him and gives him strength. He struggles to sit up, finds himself in an abandoned grove. Something is missing. There is a hollow inside of him, as if he has lost a piece of his heart.

This is something he cannot live without. He does not know what it is or where to find it, but find it he must.

However long it takes.

ABOUT THE AUTHOR

M Pepper Langlinais is an award-winning screenwriter, produced playwright, and published author. M holds a Master of Arts in Writing, Literature and Publishing and a Bachelor of Science in Radio-Television-Film. She has a love of Shakespeare, having both performed and taught his work, and has also interned on Hollywood film sets. M worked for Houghton Mifflin and Pearson before deciding to devote her full time to her own writing. She lives in Livermore, California.